# The
# BAKER STREET
# JURORS

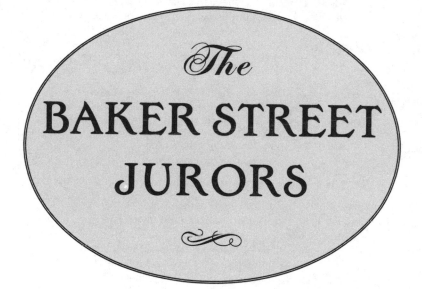

# The
# BAKER STREET
# JURORS

## MICHAEL ROBERTSON

**MINOTAUR BOOKS**
A Thomas Dunne Book
New York

A THOMAS DUNNE BOOK FOR MINOTAUR BOOKS.
An imprint of St. Martin's Publishing Group.

www.thomasdunnebooks.com
www.minotaurbooks.com

The Library of Congress has cataloged the print edition as follows:

Names: Robertson, Michael, 1951– author.
Title: The Baker Street jurors : a Baker Street mystery / Michael Robertson.
Description: First edition. | New York : Minotaur Books, 2016. | Series: The Baker Street letters ; 5 | "A Thomas Dunne book."
Identifiers: LCCN 2015050066| ISBN 9781250060068 (hardcover) | ISBN 9781466865273 (ebook)
Subjects: LCSH: 221B Baker Street (London, England : Imaginary place)—Fiction. | Lawyers—England—London— Fiction. | Murder—Investigation—Fiction. | Holmes, Sherlock—Fiction. | Letter writing—Fiction. | Brothers— Fiction. | BISAC: FICTION / Mystery & Detective / General. | GSAFD: Mystery fiction.
Classification: LCC PS3618.O31726 B347 2016 | DDC 813/.6—dc23
LC record available at http://lccn.loc.gov/2015050066

Our books may be purchased in bulk for promotional, educational, or business use. Please contact your local bookseller or the Macmillan Corporate and Premium Sales Department at 1-800-221-7945, extension 5442, or by e-mail at MacmillanSpecialMarkets@macmillan.com.

First Edition: July 2016

10  9  8  7  6  5  4  3  2  1

*For my father, Bill McKinley*

# ACKNOWLEDGMENTS

My thanks to my editor, Marcia Markland, and assistant editor, Quressa Robinson; production editor, Elizabeth Curione; designer, Nicola Ferguson; publicist, Shailyn Tavella; jacket designer, David Baldeosingh Rotstein; and copy editor, NaNá Stoelzle, at Thomas Dunne Books/St. Martin's Press.

My thanks also to my agent, Kathleen Nishimoto, at William Morris Endeavor, and Laura Bonner, for international rights.

WATSON, YOU ARE A BRITISH JURY, AND I NEVER
MET A MAN WHO WAS MORE EMINENTLY FITTED
TO REPRESENT ONE.

—Sherlock Holmes,
*The Adventure of the Abbey Grange*,
by Sir Arthur Conan Doyle

# The
# BAKER STREET
# JURORS

# Prologue

It was no ordinary cricket bat.

Made of English willow, harvested at its prime from a Suffolk preserve and air-dried without a single knot or blemish, it bore the emblem of the England cricket team, and it had won more international championships for England than any piece of sporting equipment in modern history.

It was Liam McSweeney's cricket bat—and there was blood on it.

Chief Inspector Wembley didn't touch the bat, but only stared. His heart was breaking.

He shook his head very, very slowly from side to side, and said, "He can't have done it. Dear Lord God in Heaven, let someone please tell me a reason why he can't possibly have done it."

The constable standing next to the cricket bat—which lay only partially concealed, under a rosebush in the east garden of the mansion in Hampstead—nodded his agreement with Wembley's sentiment, and said, "Not McSweeney. Surely not McSweeney."

But then the constable volunteered what he knew, "Your forensics officer said it's his bat, his fingerprints, his footprints, his house, and his wife. Pending lab confirmation, of course. I mean, except for the house part. And the wife part. Don't need the lab to confirm those."

Wembley straightened his posture and put on his official face, which was like steel on a cold day.

"You were the first officer on the scene?" said Wembley.

"No, sir. That was Sergeant Thackeray. He was so upset when he saw the condition of the body that—well, he was just overcome, sir. We sent him back to the station for some counseling."

"That'll happen to a rookie," said Wembley.

"He's actually been on the force a few years. But we're a quiet neighborhood. We don't get much of this sort of thing. Not like this, anyway."

"Show me," said Wembley.

They walked on ceramic pavers across the side lawn of the Hampstead mansion, with the morning dew still shining on the green grass. At the far end they reached a wrought-iron fence with a gate, and just inside that gate, the Scotland Yard forensics team was huddled around something covered with a tarp.

Inspector Wembley approached.

Helen O'Shea, the lead forensics officer, lifted the tarp. O'Shea's expression, conditioned by twenty years at her job, was always professionally stoic. But the constable stepped back. And Inspector Wembley himself managed to stand his ground for only perhaps two seconds before he too chose to look away.

"It's textbook," said O'Shea. "If you want a perfect illustration of injuries consistent with a crime of passion, this is it."

"All of it from the cricket bat?" said Wembley.

"Yes," said O'Shea, "and from someone who knew how to swing it, too. The first blow, the one that incapacitated her, was a classic batsman's uppercut. The next one—overhead, which I guess isn't exactly cricket, but effective for this purpose—did her in. All the ones that followed were gratuitous."

Wembley gestured for O'Shea to cover the body back up.

"The gate was locked?" he said.

"Yes."

"Any footprints on the other side?"

"No. The only footprints are between here and McSweeney's house. Hers go only one way. His—the footprints of the size-ten male, weighing about a hundred and eighty pounds, with a pattern that matches a style that McSweeney likes, given what we found in his closet—go in both directions."

The constable, still standing back from the covered body, shook his head, and said again, "Not McSweeney. Surely not McSweeney."

O'Shea looked up. "Why does everyone keep saying that?"

"You don't take your sports all that seriously then, do you, Helen?" said Wembley.

O'Shea shrugged. "I do. But if the shoe fits . . . and it does . . ."

Now a uniformed officer shouted from the side yard. "Inspector?"

Wembley turned. The sergeant pointed toward the street in front of the house.

"Here they come!"

"Bloody hell," said Wembley.

He glared at the arriving media vans. The body was only hours cold, and the BBC was already here.

1

SEVEN MONTHS LATER

It was early spring, so early that it didn't really feel that way. As Lois exited the Marylebone tube station and turned the corner onto Baker Street, she saw fluffy white clouds high over the trees of Regents Park. But they were gliding on a cold northeast wind.

Lois zipped up her parka and walked less than halfway up the 200 block. She stopped at the newsstand in front of the Dorset National Building Society—just across the street from the French patisserie and a few doors down from the Beatles memorabilia store.

She didn't want a newspaper. But she knew she probably needed to pick up a coffee. She took a moment to look up at the second-story window above her, to be sure. She saw no light in the window.

So yes, better get the coffee.

"A large?" said Bob, who ran the newsstand.

"Yes, and put gobs of sugar in it, too. Not for me, of course, I don't need it."

"Oh, I say we all need a little of it," said Bob.

Lois was fifty or a few years more, rather short, more than a little rotund, and not concerned about it, despite all the public service announcements. But she'd given up sugar in her own coffee long ago.

She glanced at the news headlines as Bob poured the very dark brew. There were the usual domestic and worldly disputes. But the dominant story—in all but *Barron's*, which gave it second billing to something more staid—was from the world of sports, and of murder.

"McSweeney Must Play," said one headline, in an English daily tabloid.

"McSweeney Must Pay," said another headline. Lois looked closer at that one. It was from a New Zealand weekly. She wondered if it might be a typo.

Lois paid for the coffee and tried not to spill any through the tiny aperture in the lid as she opened the door at Dorset House.

Two American tourists, their noses pressed up against the glass wall of the entrance, delayed her. Lois felt sorry for the puzzled middle-aged man, who obviously was not clear on the concept of March weather in London and was rubbing his bare arms as he spoke. His wife at least had a sweater.

"Is this the place where Sherlock Holmes . . ."

"No," said Lois. "Your best bet is the museum up the street."

"But that doesn't make sense," said the man. "The museum is almost at the other end of the block. The address 221B wouldn't be up there, it would be right—"

"Yes, I know, and I'm sorry about that," said Lois. "And for what it's worth, the Royal Mail delivery service agrees with you. But you won't find Sherlock Holmes here. This is Dorset House, and all the tenants of Dorset House are strictly business. Especially these days. Cheers."

Lois knew that answer would not satisfy them—it wouldn't have satisfied her, if she'd been in their shoes—but it couldn't be helped. She went into the Dorset House lobby and walked quickly across the marble floor to the security guard's station.

The security guard was a white-haired, wiry man in his seventies, who looked up from his sports section as Lois approached. "Good morning, Mr. Hendricks," said Lois.

"*The Daily Sun* has it spot-on, don't you think?" said Hendricks.

"Regarding?" said Lois.

Hendricks held up the paper and displayed the page-one headline that Lois had already seen: "McSweeney Must Play!"

"The New Zealand paper has a headline just like that," said Lois. "Except theirs says 'Pay,' not 'Play.'"

"That's because the Kiwis want to win the championship themselves. He's innocent until proven guilty, ain't he?"

"Yes," said Lois, and now the headline made sense. The Kiwis had international cricket ambitions of their own. And, like siblings, the competition between England and former members of the British Empire was always more fierce than between complete strangers.

"Well, there you have it then," said Hendricks. "They

must let him play in the championship. They must! You don't convict an entire nation over one man's indictment, is what I always say, and *The Daily Sun* says it, too, right here. So unless he's found guilty, the International Cricket Council will let him play, right?"

"I suppose."

"Well, they bloody well better," said Hendricks. "I put ten quid on England winning this year. But it won't happen without McSweeney."

"I'm sure you're right," said Lois, though she had no idea. "Have you seen Nigel yet this morning?"

"No."

"Oh my. I was afraid of that."

"It's not the end of the world."

"Well, that's easy for you to say, Mr. Hendricks," said Lois. "I'm worried about him. It was so sudden—from his point of view—and he just hasn't seemed himself since he came back."

"Looks the same to me," said Hendricks.

"Well, the hurt is on the inside, of course."

"Bollocks. Nothing that a good rugby scrum won't knock out of you. He just got soft there, staying across the pond for so long. Why, back in the day, I can tell you things . . ."

"You often do, Mr. Hendricks. And quite shocking they are, too."

Hendricks grinned, showing only a few missing teeth—which, he often said, made him not a bad catch for a man in his seventies, especially one who was still quite capable in other areas as well.

Now he winked at Lois. "No, I don't think I've shocked you quite yet, miss. But give me a chance and I will."

"No call for that, Mr. Hendricks. But wait till I tell you this . . ."

Hendricks waited, his eyes widening, for Lois to lean forward and loudly whisper, "He doesn't even care about the letters anymore! He's begun to pass them off to me!"

Hendricks raised an eyebrow. And then he focused on the view afforded by Lois leaning forward.

She stood back and checked the buttons on her blouse.

"The letters are the very thing that made it possible for him to meet her in the first place, you know," she said. "If she hadn't written a letter—and if he hadn't thought it his job to respond to it—he'd never have gone to Los Angeles to save her, and fall for her, and move in with her, and all of it."

"So, he rescued a damsel in distress, so to speak, and then she got all better and flew the coop, as it were?"

"You could describe it that way. I'm not sure I would, but you can if you like."

"Damned damsels in distress. Always up and doing things like that. Why, I remember, back in the day, when I—"

"Thank you so much for your willingness to share, Mr. Hendricks, but I believe you have told me before . . ."

"Well, it wasn't so long ago, you know," and he was leaning toward her again.

"I don't doubt you, Mr. Hendricks. And don't you dare mention to Nigel that I said anything!"

Hendricks assured her by drawing an index finger across his lips.

Lois checked her blouse again, walked across the quiet

lobby, and got into the lift. It was still early, not yet nine o'clock, and so the Dorset National Bank employees—who occupied all the first-floor office space at Dorset House—had not yet arrived.

The second floor belonged to Baker Street Law Chambers. And when the lift doors opened on that floor this morning, Lois found it even quieter than the downstairs lobby.

Diagonally across from the lift was Lois's desk. She was both secretary and administrative assistant. And receptionist. And barrister's clerk. The barrister—the only one officially a member of Baker Street Law Chambers at the moment— was Reggie Heath, Q.C. His office was the large one on the opposite wall. Lois knew he wasn't there. Reggie was on his extended honeymoon holiday. She was not to call him with trivia. Neither was she to call him with emergencies. She was not to call him at all.

Farther down the corridor was the smaller office—the office of Reggie's younger brother—Nigel Heath, solicitor. To the extent that he could, within the different legal authorizations of their different legal professions, Nigel was to hold the fort in Reggie's absence.

In Lois's opinion, especially so when she first came to work for them a few years ago, the personality differences between the two brothers suited their choice of occupations rather neatly.

Reggie, the more flamboyant, aggressive, and generally alpha-male-ish, had become a barrister, and rather early in life, too. Nigel, the more studious and inward—though given to sudden bursts of nonconformity and rebellion—had, through various twists and turns, become a solicitor.

But then, when Reggie located his new chambers on Baker Street, and the letters had begun to arrive—letters for which Nigel had always had more of an affinity than Reggie—Nigel had begun to change.

Coming out of his shell, is how Lois had described it. Rather late in life, in his thirties to be sure—but coming out of it, just the same.

What seemed to have made all the difference was the very first letter he had responded to. That letter had taken him to Los Angeles—where he met Mara Ramirez, a young woman who had written a letter twenty years earlier, as a child, to Sherlock Homes. And when it was all resolved, he had remained there with that young woman in California.

But now Nigel had returned to London. And it seemed to Lois that he had begun to revert to his old ways. Before Los Angeles. Before Mara Ramirez. Before the letters.

Four weeks ago, Reggie Heath and Laura Rankin had gotten married. Nigel was best man. He had flown out from Los Angeles, where he had been living the past two years with Mara. But Mara had not come to London to attend the wedding with Nigel.

"I don't want to talk about it," Nigel had said repeatedly, until Lois finally had the good sense to stop asking. But she had her theory. Such things are not unusual around the time of weddings—relationships can heat to a boil, one way or another, and not just for the star participants.

So Nigel had remained in London, but no longer having a flat in the city, he had taken up residence in the empty law office, and gone back to work as a solicitor in the bargain.

His office door was closed at the moment, and the blinds

were shut, and as Lois had already seen from the street, the lights were out. But she was sure he would be there. He was always there, these days. Day and night. Well, not all night. He was away at the pub for hours in the evening, especially for the darts and snooker competitions. But except for that, he'd been camping out in his office for weeks now.

Lois walked up with the large coffee in her hand and she rapped on the office door.

"Wake up, Mr. Heath!"

No response. She took the plastic lid off the large coffee, still hot enough to steam, and she blew on it lightly to help the aroma on its way. She rapped again on the door.

"Wake up and smell it, please!" she shouted. Quite cheerily, but it was a shout, even so. She put the coffee down on the floor, just to the side so that it wouldn't spill when Nigel finally opened his door.

Then she went back to her desk to see what might have arrived in the mail that absolutely required her attention. As she sat down, she heard the office door creak open. She didn't bother to look up. She heard a sigh, and then what might have been a slurp, and then the sound of bare feet walking down the corridor to the loo.

Lois focused on the two in-baskets on her desk. One was for the law chambers. That in-basket contained no more than half a dozen letters, and there was no hurry about those, given that Reggie Heath, Q.C., was away.

But the other incoming basket, the one not for the law chambers, was overflowing.

And every one of those letters was addressed to Sherlock Holmes at 221B Baker Street.

Or to Mr. Sherlock Holmes, Consulting Detective, at 221B Baker Street.

Or to Mr. Sherlock Holmes and Dr. John Watson, or to Mr. Sherlock Holmes c/o Sir Arthur Conan Doyle, or to any number of combinations thereof.

Lois began to sort through them all. This was mandatory. The lease agreement with Dorset House made it so. Because of its address, Baker Street Chambers was required to respond to the letters that people from around the world wrote to Sherlock Holmes, despite the fact that even if he were real, he would be long since dead and buried.

Most of the letters—like the one from an elderly woman whose cat had gone missing, or the ones written by schoolchildren because their teacher told them to— required only a form letter in response, saying that Sherlock Holmes had retired to Sussex to keep bees.

But now Lois saw one that was different.

She gasped.

This one she did not set aside. This one could not be ignored.

It read:

"Dear Mr. Sherlock Holmes:

You have been selected for jury service.

Her Majesty's Royal Comprehensive Database service lists you as residing at 221B Baker Street in Marylebone, and shows that you are more than eighteen years of age and that you are an English citizen with no felony convictions within the past ten years. You are therefore eligible for mandatory service as a juror.

Mandatory means that your service is not optional.

You are required to attend on Monday, the 24th of March, at the London Central Criminal Courts building.

You are not merely invited. It is not a party. It is jury service. You are required to attend.

If you feel that you have received this summons in error, or if any of the details of your eligibility are incorrect, you may file a letter of appeal within five (5) days of the postmark of this letter.

Please be prompt.

Warning: A failure to appear is a criminal offense punishable by imprisonment and/or a fine of up to £1000.

Lois stared back at the jury summons, picked it up, read it again, checked Her Royal Majesty's seal at the top to make sure it was real, checked that the same seal existed on the envelope that had contained this dreadful missive, and sighed—yes, it was real.

And, of course, the narrow deadline for objecting to it and filing an appeal had already passed.

Someone would have to deal with this.

Lois looked up from her desk. Nigel's office door was open now. He was back from the loo. Quite possibly more or less awake. Lois picked up the Sherlock Holmes jury summons—and also a handful of mail addressed actually to Nigel—and she walked down the corridor to his office.

She paused at the open doorway and looked in. Nigel wasn't a tidy man by nature—but Lois could see that he was making an effort. There were only two or three Mars bar wrappers on his desk.

Nigel looked up. He hadn't shaved yet this morning. Or yesterday morning, either, apparently. He was thirty-six years of age, somewhat under six feet tall to the same extent that his brother Reggie was somewhat over, never quite as successful with the ladies as his brother was, but not bad looking, either—and if Lois, perpetually optimistic, had not been twenty years his senior, she would have at least entertained a notion.

Nigel's desk was covered in legal documents—wills and trusts, leasehold agreements, and legal boilerplate. As a solicitor—rarely taking a litigation to court, as a barrister could do, but always just hammering away (though quite effectively) to create impregnable contracts—he had complained to Lois more than once that he needed a change. Some variety. Either give up the law altogether, or get his barrister's certification, as Reggie had done years ago. It was coming to that; something would have to change, one way or the other.

He had his head down now in those documents, and Lois put the jury summons in front of him, with its bold red letters and Crown Court insignia.

Nigel looked up, saw that insignia, and laughed. "So they got you, did they? Happens to all of us, Lois, sooner or later. And probably sooner; there are some very troublesome trials coming up, and I hear the Crown is having trouble rounding up enough victims. I mean, jurors."

"Look closer," said Lois. "It's not for me."

Nigel froze. "Please don't say it's for me."

"Not for you, either," said Lois, and she tapped her index finger emphatically on the name and address. Nigel looked at the name on the summons, and then at Lois. "Seriously?" he said.

"Nothing on it that says April Fools," said Lois. "And it's not yet April. Should I write back and tell them they can't put a character of fiction on jury service?"

"No, that will just dig the hole deeper. These things are done by computer. You can't argue with them. Maybe some prankster put the name Sherlock Holmes on a registered voters' list and the system has just now randomly picked it up. Or maybe they're so desperate for jurors they're just sending now to every address to which the Royal Mail delivers. And since the Royal Mail has been delivering letters to Sherlock Holmes to this building ever since it was put up sixty years ago—well, there you are. Sooner or later, the insistence of Sherlock Holmes fans that he is real was bound to cross paths with the Crown's need for jurors."

"Then what do we do?"

"Nothing."

"But it says they'll assess a thousand-pound fine for failure to appear."

"Let them. Good luck finding a Mr. Sherlock Holmes to collect it from. Just be glad that they haven't come for you yet. One of the trials starting at the Old Bailey is the McSweeney murder case. The media is all over it, and it will go on for weeks. And then there's the Switcombe insider trading case. Dry as the desert, and just as hard to get through. And then there's a civil trial that—well, I won't even describe it to you. You don't even want to know. In any case, Sherlock Holmes, being a character of fiction, is not required to serve."

"But what will happen when he doesn't report? Won't they send the . . . jury police or something to collect him?"

"I've never heard of it happening, but it would be entertaining to see them try in this instance. Too bad my brother won't be back by then—they'd probably figure that he is close enough, at least in appearance, and cart him off in handcuffs."

Nigel looked in the direction of the wastebasket, at the far corner of the room, next to the street window.

"This will be a three-point shot," he said.

He was about to crumple the Sherlock Holmes jury summons into a ball.

"Wait!" said Lois. "You mustn't wad it up!"

Nigel stopped. "You're right," he said. "That wouldn't show proper respect for Her Majesty's Courts Service."

Lois had spoken just in time. Nigel laid the still-pristine summons flat on the desk in front of him.

And then he folded it lengthwise down the middle, made two more angular folds at one end, and two additional creases lengthwise for air-worthiness.

"For shame!" said Lois. "You mustn't! It's an official jury summons!"

"Sorry," said Nigel. "But it is indeed an official jury summons—addressed to Sherlock Holmes—and so I must."

Nigel raised the paper airplane and lofted it lightly in the direction of the wastebasket. It flew reasonably on course for about two meters—and then it caught a draft and vanished from view.

"Bollocks," said Nigel, getting up from his desk. "I didn't know the window was open."

"And now," said Lois, quite sincerely, "you have not only desecrated an official Crown Court document, but you have also littered."

They both went to the window and looked down. But there was nothing to be done. Wherever it had gone, it was no longer within view.

Nigel shrugged and went back to his desk. Lois followed, still annoyed.

"Serving on a jury is a civic duty, Mr. Heath, and I for one would be proud to do it!"

"You're absolutely right," said Nigel. "Unfortunately, they don't assemble juries by taking volunteers. In my experience, the more you want to be on a jury, the less likely they are to seat you—and the more you don't want to be on one, the more certain they are to force you to be. When I was in law school, I desperately wanted to get on a jury to see how the jurors thought. And so the court never accepted me. But now that I've been in practice long enough to have had my fill of juries, I'm sure they'd rope me in without question if they got the chance."

"Well, I expect you'll be safe this time. I'm sure they only send one notice per address."

"Not so. Laura got a summons once for her cat, presumably because of a veterinarian's list. Once an address gets in the database, anyone whose name is associated with it in any way could . . ."

Nigel stopped suddenly. He looked at Lois, she at him, and then they both looked at the unopened stack of incoming mail on Nigel's own desk.

Nigel peeked gingerly through the stack. And there he

saw it—on the top edge of one unopened envelope was the emblem of Her Majesty's Courts Service. A jury summons.

And this one was addressed to Nigel Heath.

"Bloody hell," said Nigel.

"There! You see?" said Lois. "Be careful what you don't wish for!"

Outside, at Bob's Newsstand on Baker Street, Bob stood behind the counter and watched a paper airplane drift down and settle lightly just in front of his display of daily tabloids.

For a brief moment Bob considered picking up the aerodynamic document—but from the bright official colors on it, he was pretty sure he knew what it was. He had been on jury duty a couple of times before, himself. Of course, this summons wasn't for him—but even so, he feared somehow that just by touching it he might acquire some responsibility that he just did not need right now.

So he hesitated, and did not immediately rush out from behind his newsstand to rescue it.

And then a breeze picked the summons off the ground and sent it kiting on down Baker Street.

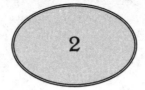

2

It was Monday morning on the day that Nigel was to report to jury service.

Nigel was up early. He wanted to get to the Old Bailey before the full crowd of potential jurors arrived, so he could get a seat in the main waiting room. Late arrivals would have to wait on the benches in the corridors, which had no cushions and no backs.

He had shaved. He'd put on a relatively clean shirt. There was no need to dress up, but no point in making a show of being unusually slovenly, either. He had seen prospective jurors try that gambit before, and it never worked.

Besides, he knew he already had an out. After all, he was a lawyer.

Nigel exited Dorset House and went immediately to Bob's Newsstand for his coffee. With luck, being so early would mean the coffee was fresh. Lois always seemed to manage it.

He watched Bob pour the coffee, saw the thickness of it, and realized that he would never be that lucky.

And Bob seemed upset. Perhaps that was why he was serving up coffee that looked as though it were left over from the day before. Even though the day before was Sunday.

"Have you seen the McSweeney headlines?" said Bob. "It's an outrage, ain't it?"

"What is?" said Nigel.

"Why, just like it says here in the papers—that anyone could even think McSweeney did it!"

Nigel nodded patiently. There had to be a time when Bob made the coffee fresh. But he would probably never discover it if he was rude to the man.

"At least it's a change," said Nigel. "To see the media in a frenzy to acquit rather than convict. They haven't been so much on the defense side of things since that young English au pair got convicted in Boston. And then when the American judge finally agreed with them and threw the conviction out, they didn't like that, either. The usual clamor is to convict. Like the Maxwell case. Or that American woman who was subjected to a jury-less trial in Italy."

"If you say so. But what I say is, it's an outrage."

"It always is. The tabloids are like the street mob in an American Western, coming with ropes and rifles to grab the legal system and string it up. And there's no sheriff guarding the door. Except the jury. And who protects the jury?"

Bob rubbed his forehead. "Philosophy is not my cup of tea, Heath. I just wanted to talk about sports. Innocent until proven guilty is all I know about the law. Like this—see, what it says right here . . ."

Bob held the paper out, and Nigel had no choice. He had to look.

It was an editorial:

"If the three-time England cricket team international champion is convicted of murder, then of course he should not play. If he is found guilty of some lesser charge, then that can be considered according to the weight it deserves. But at this moment, Liam McSweeney has not been convicted of anything at all. And along with England's recently established tradition of finally winning at international cricket, there is an even more important tradition, of much longer standing: innocent until proven guilty. Surely Liam McSweeney is entitled to this as much as any man, and surely the Cricket Council will not deny Mr. McSweeney—or England itself—the privilege of attempting to win a fourth international championship unless and until he is actually convicted."

Nigel read it and nodded politely. "Quite right, and well put," he said. "Oh, and Bob—I'll be doing early hours for a while, so if you don't mind—when do you make your first batch in the morning?"

"Ten minutes ago, just like yours," said Bob.

Nigel absorbed the discouraging implications of that and hurried on his way, hoping to still get to the courthouse before everyone else.

But no. There was construction on one of the underground lines, and his train was delayed. When he finally ran up to the courthouse, the narrow jurors' entrance already had a queue that snaked outside, into the cold wind, and halfway down the side alley.

Nigel took his position at the end of that line as more stragglers hurried up from both ends of the alley.

A tall, fiftyish man, clean-shaven, with a thin, aquiline nose stepped into line behind Nigel. "Bloody hell," he said. "Is this really the jurors' queue?"

"I'm afraid so," said Nigel. "It's enough to make you want to commit a crime of your own, just to get inside and be warm."

"At least it isn't raining," chirped a woman nearby, and then the whole line groaned aloud in unison, because the moment it was said, the first spots began to appear on the ground.

One hundred umbrellas went up all at once.

"Ow," said a woman somewhere ahead in the line, followed by a "sorry, miss," from the reckless gentleman who had done it.

And now that rain was added to the cold and wind, the queue seemed to jostle forward a foot or so—and then it immediately stopped.

Nigel estimated this process would repeat itself for another twenty minutes or so before he reached the front of the queue.

But he was wrong. It took twice that.

Finally he reached the entrance.

"Jury summons, please?" said the uniformed woman at the check-in.

Nigel presented his jury summons. She checked it against a list.

"I have my ID here somewhere," said Nigel. "I think. If I forgot it, do I get to go home and come back next year?"

"Nice try, but a summons and a heartbeat is sufficient," said the woman. "You are now jury candidate two-oh-five."

She gave Nigel his number stub, waved him in, and called for the next in line.

"Oh, that's an interesting name," Nigel heard her say to the tall man, who was next. "When you combine it with that initial."

"I get that a lot," was the response from the tall man. "And as an officer of the court, you might be interested to know that it is the same surname as a former United States Supreme Court justice."

"Carries no weight here," said the clerk. "But thank you for calling me an officer of the court. You are now jury candidate two-oh-six."

Nigel followed the juror candidates in front of him up an interior flight of stairs. They came to a halt. The Old Bailey corridor was packed. The jury assembly room itself, which Nigel knew had at least a hundred relatively comfortable cloth-covered chairs, was completely full and had overflowed its supply of potential jurors.

All the horizontal space on the hard corridor benches was taken as well. So was all the vertical space where you might lean casually back against the wall, or carefully against the glass-encased three-hundred-year-old portraits of be-wigged legal scholars. It was worse than standing room only. There was enough room in the corridor, perhaps, for one-hundred-plus pairs of feet, but not for one-hundred-plus shoulders and Guinness-fed bellies.

A voice somewhere at the far end of the corridor said, "Don't everyone exhale at the same time, or we'll all either die or get pregnant." Two or three people laughed.

Nigel didn't. Claustrophobia was beginning to set in.

Deep breath. Count the portraits of the famous lords on the walls. Deep breath again.

Wasn't working. He looked around for something else that could hold his focus.

Then he saw it.

It appeared to be either a rose or a heart or a butterfly. He couldn't see enough of it yet to be sure. But whether flora or fauna, it was located just below the belt line on the right hip of the slender woman standing directly in front of him.

And it would come into view, just for a glimpse, whenever she shifted her weight impatiently from one foot to the other.

Nigel wanted to know more. A rose, or heart, or especially a butterfly—any of those would be fine. He peered.

So long as it was not a black widow. Or a scorpion. Or a dragon.

And perhaps there was another small tattoo—on her left breast, just for symmetry?

"What are you looking at?"

She had turned. Nigel looked away too late; he was caught, and he knew it.

In for a penny, in for a pound. He tried an obvious lie with a smile.

"I wasn't."

"Wasn't what?"

"Wasn't looking at . . . whatever you think I was looking at."

She was a woman in her midthirties. Or perhaps as much as forty, it was difficult to tell—she was rather slender, hair cut short with half a nod toward style and half toward convenience, and she wore large, round spectacles, through which she had fixed Nigel in a glare.

Altogether, she gave the impression of Lisbeth Salander growing up to become Annie Hall. She wore a youngish woman's top, and when she turned to face him, Nigel thought he did indeed catch a glimpse of another tattoo, though he couldn't see what this one was, either.

But Nigel knew he had not only been caught looking, but also shot down in flames for trying to follow up. If he could have backed up and blended into the crowd, he would have—but he couldn't. There was no room to move.

"Were you trying to see if I have a tattoo there?"

"Tattoo where?" said Nigel, almost immediately realizing that wasn't his best possible response.

And then he was saved by a loud announcement from a court steward. "All jurors in group 1B, please proceed to court number thirteen at the end of the corridor."

There was a general murmur as everyone looked at their summons notices. Nigel, still pinned by the woman's wary stare, held his breath—and then, at last, she looked away from him to check the numbers on her own summons.

The steward read the announcement again, this time more loudly and with gestures to point the direction, and a throng of jurors—the woman with the tattoo among them—began to move in that direction.

Nigel checked his own summons. No, he was not in group 1B. He was in 2C.

That was certainly lucky. Saved from some prolonged embarrassment there. Nigel sighed as the woman disappeared into the courtroom at the far end of the hallway.

There was some breathing room now in the corridor, but only a little, with group 2C jurors moving back and forth between the corridor, the loo, and the public canteen—from which the tall man who had spoken to Nigel earlier emerged now with a cellophane-packaged sandwich.

As Nigel surveyed all this, it occurred to him that perhaps there was actually a juror surplus. Perhaps his own group would be sent home.

Directly behind Nigel was a midtwenties man wearing old, ragged, and very dirty clothes. He was muttering to himself, or pretending to.

Nigel looked over his shoulder at him.

"It won't work," said Nigel.

"Why not?" said the man, with perfectly lucid enunciation, but in a low voice so that no one else could hear.

"You can't pretend to be a homeless schizophrenic. For one, that won't actually disqualify you. But aside from that, the judge will immediately notice your fingernails. And if the judge is too nearsighted to see you've kept them clipped, the bailiff will notice instead, and will point it out. Either way, it won't work. You can't fake it, and if you try, the court can hold you in contempt, just as if you had deliberately come in pissed with beer."

"All my mates said they found a way out of it."

"Good luck with that," said Nigel.

And now Nigel felt just a little guilty about wanting to get out of jury duty himself. But then the steward came out to the corridor to make another announcement. Nigel's guilt quickly gave way to hope once more that his group would be sent home.

"Attention, all jurors in group 2C. Attention, all jurors in group 2C."

There was a long pause. Then . . .

"All jurors in group 2C, kindly proceed to court number thirteen."

Bloody hell, thought Nigel.

# 3

The Court 13 jury steward, a pleasant, fortyish woman of Indian extraction, opened the door to let Nigel's group into the courtroom. She pointed the jury pool toward their seating gallery—a set of fifty seats, immediately to their left, at the near wall of the courtroom.

Nigel took the first available seat he came to, next to a woman in the front row. But there was a brief distraction as several other jurors jockeyed for position, trying to guess whether one seat would make them more likely to be called for service than another.

"Just take a seat please," said the steward. "No need to be shy."

The woman next to Nigel turned to him now and said, "Is it safer back there?" Nigel looked at her. It was the woman with the tattoo.

"I mean," she said, "are you less likely to be called in the back row?"

"No," said Nigel. "They'll call us at random. And in any

case, if you've got any sort of excuse at all, you want to be called earlier rather than later. By the time they get to the final prospects, the court is usually getting desperate—at that point, they wouldn't excuse even the defendant's own mother."

"Too bad," laughed the woman. "That's what I was going to claim."

"No way they'd believe that, unless they've started prosecuting nursery schoolers as adults," said Nigel. "But you might not be called anyway. They've already got ten of the first-string jurors selected." He pointed toward the main jury section, where ten permanent chairs were already occupied, and only two were empty.

"Then what are those other chairs for?" She pointed to five empty chairs next to the main jury section.

"Those are bad news," said Nigel. "It looks like the Crown wants five alternates. That means they expect a trial of several weeks. And that probably means it's the McSweeney trial."

"Oh my," said the woman. "Well, there are just gobs of us to choose from. Perhaps you and I will be lucky and get skipped."

"Perhaps," said Nigel. "But the Crown is getting desperate; they know they won't find any jurors at all who don't know about the trial, and bloody few who don't worship McSweeney. At this point, I think they'll settle for anyone who will simply confess that they will do their best according to the evidence."

"What do you mean, 'confess'?" said the woman.

"I mean, I've seen jury selections where ninety-nine

people out of a hundred will insist that they are already prejudiced in favor of either the defense or the prosecution—because they believe that will force the judge to exclude them. But judges are wise to the tactic, of course. And in practice, something magical happens to people when they are put on a jury. Almost invariably they all decide to do their jobs."

"I expect they will take me," said a male voice from the row behind them. Nigel turned to look. It was the tall man who'd been behind Nigel in the outside line. In the same row was a woman near seventy in a respectable wool coat, a man in his forties with heavily calloused hands, and a man in his midtwenties with an expensive haircut and even more expensive shoes.

"I've always wanted to be on a jury," said the tall man. "And the court will appreciate my skills in applying the rule that should be applied in all circumstantial cases."

Nigel found that remark curious. "Which is?" he said.

"When you have eliminated the impossible, whatever remains, however improbable, must be the truth."

"I've heard that somewhere before," said the woman with the tattoo.

"So have I," said Nigel. "But not as a legal concept, exactly."

"I want to do my duty, too, of course," said the woman with the tattoo. "But I rather hope they don't put me on a jury."

"Sorry to hear that," said Nigel, out loud, and she gave him a quizzical look. "I meant," said Nigel, "I'm sure you'd be an excellent juror."

"Hmm," she said, and then she added, "I've put in for a hardship excuse. But I don't think I'll get it."

"I don't mind if they take me," said the older woman seated behind them, "but I don't think they will." She was of a pensioner's age, less than average height, perhaps an inch or so shorter than she had been in her youth, with a white woolen cap pulled over hair that still had traces of its original red, and alert blue eyes that had lost nothing with the years.

"Why would they not?" said Nigel.

"I'd rather not say," she replied. And then she added, "As my late husband used to say, never let them see you sweat. And it will be sad if they don't take me, because this will be the last year I can do it—unless they raise the maximum age limit. I think it's foolish to exclude people just because they're over seventy, don't you? We aren't all doddering fools. And some of us dribble only a little."

"I agree," said Nigel. "They don't have that restriction in the States. Regarding age or dribbling, either one."

"Well, I'm not going to move just to serve," she said. "So they'd better take me while they can."

"Well," said the man with the very expensive shoes, "they'd bloody well better not take me. I've put in for an excuse. I'm going to Ibiza next week, for god's sake."

There was just a bit more bustle now from the back row, and then, finally, the gallery of prospective jurors was full. The steward smiled victoriously and exited through a door behind the judge's bench.

For a moment, Nigel felt as though he was in a public school class with the teacher away. His entire group of prospective jurors was unattended, and free to misbehave. Except, of course, for the presence of the rather large bailiff—two-hundred-fifty-pounds, well over six feet tall, standing stoically at the opposite end of the judge's bench.

And then the steward returned, and the bailiff told everyone to rise.

The judge—tall, thin, and well into his sixties—entered and sat down at his bench. He nodded quickly to the two tables of barristers—defense and prosecution—at the center of the courtroom. Then he turned to face the jury pool with an expression that would have seemed almost avuncular, if not for the formal white wig above it.

"Good morning," he began. "I am Mr. Justice Allen. The very patient woman who has been assisting you in the corridor is our court steward, Ms. Sreenivasan, and the imposing gentleman to my left is our court bailiff, Mr. Walker. They will be here for the duration of this trial, and I am very grateful to have their assistance; you will be too if you are selected as jurors for this trial.

"In a few moments, I will ask each of you a few basic questions regarding your ability to serve as unbiased jurors in a case that has garnered an inordinate amount of publicity and that involves strong feelings in the public at a national level. But this is not like an American trial, with lawyers haggling forever over who gets to be on the jury and who does not. This is an English trial, and you will be an English jury, chosen at random, the fairest and most objective method in the world—so the court's questions for you will be brief and to the point. And I know that each of you will answer honestly."

The judge paused for a moment, making eye contact with the group of juror candidates, and added, "You may all now nod in the affirmative."

They all did so.

"Now," said the judge, "I mentioned the tremendous publicity surrounding this trial, and although I am quite reluctant to yield to such fuss, I have learned through hard experience that I must now take it into consideration. We have already had one mistrial due to juror misconduct with a member of the press, and one before that due to an allegation of juror intimidation. We will not have such annoyances in this trial. We are taking some precautions to make sure of it. And the first of those is that this jury shall remain anonymous. Your names have been recorded on the list that I have in front of me, which I share only with my bailiff and our steward. No one else has access to them, most especially the media. From this point forward, you will be identified only by the number that has been assigned to you. I cannot stop you from using your own names in conversations between each other, and so I won't try. But if you are selected for this jury, you will be under strict instructions not to reveal that fact to the public, and not to communicate with the media in any way whatsoever. Doing so could, in certain circumstances, cause you to be charged with contempt of court. Am I making myself clear?"

The jurors, having caught on to the routine, all nodded in the affirmative.

"Very good," said the judge. "As you can see, we have already selected ten of our twelve primary jurors. Let's see how quickly we can select the remaining two. Ms. Sreenivasan will now read a random number from the candidate jury pool, and I will ask one or two simple questions. Nothing to worry about, I assure you—just answer honestly."

There was as much suspense now as if it were the lottery.

"Jury candidate number one-ninety-seven," announced Ms. Sreenivasan.

The fortyish man with the calloused hands stood up in the row behind Nigel.

"Candidate one-ninety-seven," said the judge, "Have you seen coverage of the case of Crown versus McSweeney in the newspapers, or the television, or other media?"

"Yes, I have."

"Can you ignore anything you have already read or heard regarding this case and decide the issues submitted to you according to the evidence presented at trial, and nothing else?"

"I would do my best," said the man.

"That's good enough. Please take a seat in the primary jury section."

The man did so, and Ms. Sreenivasan selected another number.

"Jury candidate two-oh-eight," she announced.

The man with the very expensive shoes stood up from the back row.

"I have applied to be excused," he said, before the judge could even ask a question.

"Won't do him any good," whispered Nigel to the woman with the tattoo. "He'll be a juror."

"Why?" she said. "Because he doesn't want to be?"

"Exactly," said Nigel.

The judge shuffled some papers, got some assistance from Ms. Sreenivasan, and found the document he was looking for. He looked at the written request for perhaps two seconds.

"Denied," said the judge. "You may take a seat in the primary section."

"But . . ."

The judge looked up, and the man stopped in mid-sentence

"Denied," said the judge again.

Ms. Sreenivasan escorted the man with the expensive shoes to the twelfth seat in the primary jury section.

"At this point," whispered Nigel, "They're settling for pretty much anyone with a pulse."

"Now then," said the judge. "We have selected our twelve primary jurors. But we need alternates as well. So in a moment we shall call numbers for five possible alternates. But first, in the interests of time, I'm going to ask the remaining candidates for a show of hands. You are all being considered for a trial that is listed on the docket as the Crown versus McSweeney. Have any of you seen anything on the telly or in the newspapers related to accusations against Liam McSweeney?"

Several hands went clearly up, and several more were tentative.

"Don't be shy," said the judge. "It's not a crime if you have."

Now hands went up for every juror except two—the tall man sitting behind Nigel, and a man in the back row, who was still wearing his raincoat in the warm courtroom.

The judge looked in that direction, and then he looked at his list.

"Jury candidate number . . . one-eighty-nine?" said the judge, looking at the man in the back row. "You have not seen any news coverage regarding the matter at hand?"

"No, my lord. Not one bit."

"Have you been out of the country, then? Or off the planet in some way?"

"I . . . no, my lord. I have simply been very careful to avoid such information."

"Why?"

"On the chance that I might be called for jury duty."

"So you have been preserving your . . . jury virginity, as it were . . . on the random chance that you might be called for this specific case?"

"Ah . . . yes. I suppose you could put it that way."

"I see," said the judge. "Rather unusual. Let me just ask you this: Do you believe that you can be a fair and impartial juror in this case and perform your deliberations, should we reach that stage, based solely on the evidence and rules of law presented to you in this courtroom?"

"Absolutely."

"Very well," said the judge. But then he sighed deeply— and hesitated.

The tall juror candidate seated immediately behind Nigel leaned forward between Nigel and the woman with the tattoo, and whispered to them. "That one's going to be rejected," he said.

Nigel nodded in agreement.

"Jury candidate one-eighty-nine—would you mind very much?" said the judge. "Could you please unzip your mac?"

The man reluctantly unzipped his raincoat—to reveal a pullover jersey with the colors and logo of the England cricket team.

"That will do it," said Nigel to the woman with the tattoo. "The more you want to be on a jury for any specific case, whether to convict or acquit, the less the court wants you."

"But if the court rejects everyone who is favorably disposed toward Liam McSweeney, they'll never get a jury," said the woman.

"Very true. But this rejection won't be for the juror's predisposition. It will be because he tried so hard to conceal it."

And now the judge looked up from his list and said, quite matter-of-factly, "Jury candidate number one-eighty-nine, you are excused, with the thanks of the court."

The man in the England cricket team jersey sighed with disappointment and exited the jury gallery.

Now the judge looked at his list again, and he looked up at the tall man behind Nigel. "Jury candidate number . . . two-oh-six?" said the judge. "You did not raise your hand, either?"

"I don't own a telly, my lord. It's an annoyance I can't afford."

"Oh. Well, my sympathies. Or congratulations on your good sense, as the case may be. But you have read newspaper stories about the subject, I suppose?"

"No," said the man.

"Really?"

"Yes."

"Because newspapers are an annoyance you can't afford?"

"No, I can afford them well enough. I see pages of the *Sun*, and the *Mirror*, and the *Globe* and all the others flitting along the ground with every gust of wind. But I don't get my hands dirty by picking them up and reading them. I just glance at the headlines as they drift by."

"I see," said the judge. "Well, I'm going to mark that one as a yes. Glancing at the headlines is all that many people do anyway, which is even more problematic than reading the stories, because the headlines are twisted to begin with, and then one fills in the rest of the stories out of one's own imagination. So I'll just ask you the same question that I will ask of every juror: Can you ignore anything you have already read and/or imagined regarding this case and decide the issues submitted to you according to the evidence presented at trial, and nothing else?"

"Yes."

"Thank you. Please take a seat in the alternate jury box."

The tall man got up and walked to the alternate jury box. The judge nodded to Ms. Sreenivasan, who called out another number.

The widowed pensioner raised her hand, and without even being asked, she volunteered that she had seen both television coverage and newspaper articles, which she had read most thoroughly.

"Understood," said the judge. "And my only question for you is this: Can you ignore anything you have already read and/or imagined regarding this case and decide the issues submitted to you according to the evidence presented at trial, and nothing else?"

"Oh yes," she said. "I always do. I've been a juror three times in six years, and I've done that every time."

The judge took a moment. Probably wondering whether she was telling the truth or merely bragging, thought Nigel. And it's probably both.

"Thank you," said the judge to the pensioner. "Please take a seat in the alternate jury box."

She did so, taking a seat next to the tall man.

Ms. Sreenivasan called out another number, and a man in a salmon-colored Lacoste polo shirt stood up. He was almost certainly an insurance agent—Nigel had seen him passing out cards in the corridor. He said nothing that the judge found objectionable, and he was quickly seated as the third alternate.

Ms. Sreenivasan called out another number. The woman with the tattoo stood. "I have applied to be excused," she said.

The judge found her application among his papers. He pursed his lips. "Denied," he said. "You should be able to manage it. You may take your seat in the alternates section."

Nigel did not have time to wonder what the young woman would have to manage—because the next number called was his. Nigel stood and said nothing.

"And what is your excuse?" said the judge.

"None."

"Well, that's refreshing. You may take a seat . . ." The judge stopped. One of the barristers was as antsy as a child needing to pee.

"Mr. Slattery, do you have something to say?"

Henry Slattery, Q.C., was representing the Crown Prosecution Service. He was a portly man, fighting hard against middle age, and so proud of the hair that he still had growing in a crescent shape at the back of his head that he had let it get a bit too long, and locks of it got loose in little tufts that peeked out from the lower hem of his white wig.

Slattery stood, and said, "My lord, I believe I recognize this gentleman from previous contacts in court."

"Oh?" said the judge. "In what capacity? Are you a lawyer, jury candidate two-oh-five? Or just a criminal?"

"The former," said Nigel.

The judge frowned. "Solicitor or barrister?"

"He's merely a solicitor," said Slattery. "However, even so . . ."

"Yes, just a solicitor," nodded Nigel. "I merely know the law, I don't feel obliged to talk about it all that much." Nigel hoped that this remark would be taken in the spirit in which it was offered—and that the prosecutor would therefore try to excuse him from service.

And indeed, Slattery repeated his objection.

"Let's take this in chambers," said the judge.

The judge and barristers stood, and moments later, Nigel was summoned to join them in their private meeting.

Nigel was allowed to sit in one of the leather chairs in front of the judge's desk. The two opposing barristers stood on either side of him.

The barrister for the defense was William Langdon. He had a sharp face and a thin build, and a manner that colleagues had described as being that of an innocent ferret.

He tried to remain silent and maintain that innocent expression right now, as he enjoyed the discomfiture of his opponent.

The judge spoke first to the prosecutor.

"Under normal circumstances," said the judge, "I would simply grant your request, Mr. Slattery, and excuse this juror. No barrister wants some other lawyer on his jury. For one thing, they think they know the law better themselves, and for another, they have a tendency to focus on the process more than the case. So I would no more put a solicitor on a jury than I would someone actively involved in law enforcement. But these are not normal circumstances. We are having the devil of a time assembling a panel of jurors who have not already made up their minds based on what they've seen in the tabloids. We are down to our final candidates for the week and each of them, as you know, has some issue, or we would not be having this meeting."

"Yes," said Slattery. "But are you familiar with this particular candidate's history?"

"Enlighten me," said the judge.

"Nigel Heath was suspended two years ago by the Law Society, my lord. He has been reinstated since then, but even so . . ."

"And the reason for the suspension?"

"My lord, I hardly know how to put it."

"Give it a go, Mr. Slattery."

"He attempted to return a client's fee."

There was stunned silence in the room. The judge rubbed his forehead. He looked at Nigel. "All right then. Mr. Heath, you bollixed up a case and then you gave your client his money back, is that it?"

Nigel shook his head and was about to speak, but Slattery interrupted. "No, my lord," said Slattery. "It's much worse than that. He won his tort case, but after it was done, he attempted to return the commission he made to the opposing attorney's client."

Now the judge looked much more sternly at Nigel. "Is this true?"

"Yes," said Nigel. "It was a workman's slip-and-fall on fluid from a thawing chicken in the defendant's kitchen. I represented the workman, who presented himself as being incapacitated by his injuries. But one week after the case was done and the damages awarded, I ran across my client at a golf course in Scotland. He was in the foursome ahead of me, and he hit a drive that would have been remarkable even for a professional, much less a duffer with an alleged back injury. I realized then that I had won a bad case."

"Are we to accept then," said the judge, "that all this fuss was because you felt the outcome of the case was unjust to the opposing litigant?"

"Spot-on, my lord."

"We are an adversarial system, Mr. Heath. What do you suppose will become of the legal profession if all lawyers begin to take your approach to things?"

"I don't know, my lord."

The judge sighed and sat back in his chair. "Well," he said after a moment, "this is most unusual. But I don't see how it disqualifies Mr. Heath from jury duty."

Slattery did not seem satisfied. "My lord, I didn't want to mention this, but there is something more. I once opposed this man's brother, Reggie Heath, Q.C., in court, and juror two-oh-five here was present as solicitor on the case, and during the trial . . ."

"Yes?"

"And during the trial . . . during the trial, juror two-oh-five here . . ."

"Yes?"

"He made fun of me, my lord."

The judge looked at Nigel and then back at Slattery.

"He did . . . what, precisely?"

"He wrote notes during my opening and passed them to his brother, and—"

"That's allowed, Mr. Slattery, as you well know. So long as he didn't interrupt, the solicitor on the case is certainly permitted to communicate with his barrister."

"Yes, my lord, but . . ."

"But what?"

"After he passed one particular note, his brother looked in my direction and started to laugh, and only at the last possible moment managed to cover his mouth with his hand so that it was not audible."

"And?"

"The jurors saw this, my lord, looked at me, and then several of them covered their mouths as well. They were clearly stifling, my lord."

"I see," said the judge. "And you believe all this restrained mirth was at your expense?"

"I know it was."

"And that this man caused it?"

"Yes, my lord."

The judge drummed his fingers and looked at Nigel. "Well?" he said. "What about it, Heath—I mean, juror two-oh-five?"

"It's all true, my lord," said Nigel. "I am sorry about it, and if the court feels obliged to dismiss me from consideration for jury duty until next year, I will humbly accept that as my just deserts."

Slattery looked at the judge victoriously, and Nigel began to get up from his chair.

"Sit down, juror two-oh-five," said the judge. "I have two more questions for you."

Nigel sat back down.

"First—what was it that you wrote in your note that made fun of Mr. Slattery?"

"I truly was not trying to make fun, my lord. I was merely pointing out a minor flaw in his presentation."

"Which was?"

"That his fly was open."

"Ah," said the judge. "Then you were not the actual source of the mirth. You were merely the bearer of the tidings. So now—my second question. Do you, in your capacity as solicitor, currently have any pending cases scheduled before this court or that involve either Mr. Slattery or Mr. Langdon or any other participating barristers?"

Nigel sighed. He knew what this meant. "No, my lord, I do not."

"Then you are seated as alternate juror number five. And if, during this trial, you see any instances of barristers with their flies open, or wigs askew, or shoes untied, kindly do not point them out."

Back in the courtroom, the twelve primary jurors were seated in a section of permanent chairs, set apart in the courtroom by a mahogany banister. On the other side of the banister were five movable chairs for the alternate jurors. Only the seat next to the woman with the tattoo was empty. Nigel sat down next to her. With the stern bailiff standing right there, there was no more whispering.

Now the panel of jurors and alternates was complete, and the judge turned to solemnly face the entire group. "You are very special people. You are English jurors," he began. "And you have been selected for a case that has been dubbed 'the trial of the century,' which is perhaps an exaggeration, because there has already been a completely different trial of the century in this century, and I'm sure there will be more before the century is out. But the fact is that the publicity is enormous. It is overwhelming. And even though trials should not be conducted through the media, and we do what we can under our British law to prevent it, it happens anyway. We have already had one mistrial in which a juror was discovered to be running off to the pub across the street and meeting with a journalist during every lunch break. You must not do that. This is not America; our jurors should not look upon a trial as their opportunity for fifteen minutes of fame. If this trial gets to the deliberation stage and you decide to write a book about those deliberations after the trial is over, you can be held in contempt. There must be no jury nobbling. That is to say, if anyone in the media attempts to get information from you about the trial while it is taking place, or if any person should attempt to influence you, that person will be prosecuted and you will of course be tossed from the jury. And I would be forced to declare another mistrial. I don't want that; we are going to some lengths to prevent it from happening. So, please—if you are impaneled on this jury, whether as an alternate or a primary—do not under any circumstances let anyone nobble you.

"Also remember that you are an anonymous jury. This is for your own protection, both from the press, and from outside influences of all sorts. Do not tell anyone that you are on this jury. Do not tell anyone the subject matter of the trial you are on.

"And finally—and this is something that not all judges care about, but I sometimes find it a concern in my courtrooms—please remember that the Royal Courts of Justice are not a social introduction service. Jury duty is not speed dating. I'm sure by the end of this, you will all agree that the trial is not a speedy anything, but please, do not endeavor to entertain yourselves by becoming overly familiar with one another. I can't stop you, of course. There's no law against it, and I vaguely remember that it's tough out there for single people. But I can beg, and I do so now. Don't complicate things."

The bailiff nodded in silent agreement as the judge gave the jurors a stern look.

"Now I realize it has been a long morning, and it is getting close to the noon hour—but we are already running quite behind schedule, and the sooner we get started, the sooner we can conclude. So I will ask you to be content right now with just a ten-minute break for the loo—and then we'll see how far along we can get with opening statements before lunch. But remember my cautions.

"Do not discuss what you hear in this courtroom with the media. Or your friends. Or your spouses. Or your parents. Or your children. Or your dogs or your cats. Or your budgies. Do not talk to yourself on the tube on the way in. And, until such time as I may tell you to retire to the jury room and begin deliberations, if it comes to that, do not discuss this case in any way with your fellow jurors. Are there any questions?"

A young woman among the twelve primary jurors raised her hand. "May we tweet?"

"Tweet?" said the judge.

The defending barrister stood and tried to be helpful. "My lord, if I may—a tweet is a form of communication in which—"

"Please," said the judge, waving him off. "As old as you may think I look, I'll have you know that my two granddaughters are still in their teens."

He turned toward the jury. "O . . . M . . . G," he said. "I can't believe I didn't already tell you this. When I say don't talk about the case, I mean do not communicate with anyone, in any format, by any means whatsoever, and most especially social media. Am I clear?"

All of the jurors silently nodded.

"Am I clear?" said the judge, more pointedly, and loudly.

"Yes, my lord," said all the jurors in unison, like recruits at boot camp.

Satisfied, the judge now adjourned the court and exited to his chambers. Ms. Sreenivasan prompted the jurors to file out to the corridor.

The juror in expensive shoes rushed off on some self-important mission; the tall juror walked toward the opposite end of the corridor and paused to fumble for something in his pocket. The woman with the tattoo checked her mobile phone as she exited into the corridor; she was followed by the pensioner widow, who hesitated in the doorway for a moment, as if uncertain that the court had truly released them.

The judge's instructions regarding fraternization notwithstanding, Nigel intended to catch up with the woman with the tattoo. But she was too quick, and Nigel was delayed when the widow stopped in the doorway. By the time he got out of the courtroom, she was gone.

**4**

In his chambers, the judge took off his wig, sat down in the chair behind his desk, leaned his head back, and pushed thinning white hair back with his fingers, as though doing so might clear his head.

It didn't much.

He put the wig down in the center of the mahogany desk in front of him—which was wrong to do, at least for any length of time, because they lose their shape—and he stared at it.

He could hardly expect a jury to resist public pressure if he could not do so himself.

He had managed it this time. But perhaps, he thought, it was time for him to retire.

Physically, he felt fine. Physically, he felt as though he could carry on indefinitely, or at least until such time as the typical unexpected thing might occur.

But it was getting increasingly difficult to keep the faith.

On his desk, next to his wig, was a copy of *The Daily Sun*.

He looked at the headline and he sighed. Every tabloid in the country was expressing its outrage that he hadn't granted an earlier defense motion to dismiss the charges because McSweeney claimed an alibi.

From a legal standpoint, it would have been absurd to grant the motion—even the defense didn't expect that he would do so. He had ruled that the case would proceed and it would be up to the jury to decide the weight of the claimed alibi, along with all the other evidence. And the defense had known he would rule that way; they had made the motion just to show how weak they pretended to think the prosecution's case was.

But that nuance would escape the media. All that mattered is that there was a chance to set Liam McSweeney, national hero, free to play cricket in the international championship, and the court had not done so.

Just a year before, the judge had faced quite the opposite situation. A murder case in which the crime had been so outrageous that the public, whipped into a frenzy by the media, demanded an immediate conviction—even though the case against that suspect had been supported by nothing more than the word of a jailhouse informant.

This was no way to run a justice system.

The judge knew full well that this tension between the press and the law had always existed. But in recent years it seemed to have gotten so much worse. Surely it was easier a century ago, without television cameras. Surely it was easier before the lines between news and entertainment had become so blurred, and people had begun to confuse reality TV with reality itself, and voting online for their favorite performers with voting for their government. Surely it was easier before cell phone videos and Twitter and instant communication of every little thought to everyone else in the world.

What would be next? Round-the-clock television and smart phone coverage of every trial, and juries composed of everyone who wanted to subscribe, tweeting in their verdict?

The judge suddenly realized that the court steward had knocked and entered his chambers. He looked up at her and said, "Ms. Sreenivasan, do you think it is time for me to retire?"

"No, sir."

"I could, you know. I think I might like to step down, and spend my afternoons looking out on the garden and writing science fiction. What do you think of that?"

"I'll put it on next year's calendar, if you like."

"Yes," said the judge. "I think I'll call it *Hashtag: Guilty.* I'll explain it later, if you like."

"No need," she said. "I'm pretty sure I can guess it all from the title. Let's hope it remains fictional a while longer. Are you ready?"

"Give me one more moment," said the judge.

The steward exited, and the judge had one more minute alone with his thoughts.

And his main thought was this: he loved juries. He loved juries almost more than he loved the law.

In America, a jury had convicted John Gotti despite threats to their safety that were very real. What sort of courage did that take?

But never mind the very rare situation where jurors had to actually worry about their physical safety. What sort of determination and mental focus must it take to listen only to the evidence at trial and ignore everything that politicians and pundits and media and the street might say? What sort of courage did it take to make an unpopular decision and go home and acknowledge it to one's own friends and family?

It was quite annoying, in this judge's view. Every time an unpopular verdict comes in, there are calls to get rid of the jury. Or to not allow them anonymity. But the purpose of the jury is not to render popular verdicts. The purpose of the jury is not to do what the crowd in the street wants done, any more than it is to do what the prosecuting authority wants done or what the media pundits want done. The purpose of the jury is to be just, according to the evidence presented to it. Nothing more nor less than that.

Leave the bloody jury alone, thought the judge.

And he put his wig back on and returned to the courtroom.

## 5

Nigel took the underground back to Baker Street. It was midafternoon now, not yet time for the full commuter rush, and although the tube was hardly empty, it felt spacious compared to the crowd that he had been in this morning.

This wasn't Nigel's usual time to be on the tube. As he came out of the Marylebone station, he missed the live music that he normally heard during the busier hours. He entered the Dorset House lobby at Baker Street, heading directly for the lift—but Hendricks at the security station waved him over.

"Listen to this, Heath," said Hendricks, with the joy of a man seeing his strongest opinions vindicated in print. He read to Nigel from a tabloid. " 'If Mr. Justice Allen thinks the English people will stand for the persecution of a man of Liam McSweeney's caliber, whose alibi is as certain as rain in April, then—.' "

"Please," said Nigel, putting up his hands to interrupt.

"No need to give me updates, Mr. Hendricks, if you don't mind." Nigel tried to say it nicely, but Hendricks looked surprised—and perhaps a little offended. It couldn't be helped. The jury was anonymous. Nigel could hardly tell Hendricks that was the reason he didn't want to hear the Liam McSweeney news.

Nigel took the lift to the second floor. Lois was at her station and caught him as he got out. "You're back early," she said enthusiastically. "Does that mean they rejected you?"

"No. I'm on a jury."

"Oh. I'm so very sorry," said Lois, but Nigel could tell she didn't mean it. She was practically breathless with anticipation. "Which one is it?" she said. "Oh. You're not supposed to tell me that, are you?"

"No."

"Just a hint?"

"No. You wanted me to do my duty, Lois. And now I'm doing it, and I'll do it properly."

"Oh, of course," said Lois. "I was just testing you, you know."

"Uh-huh." Nigel went into his office and closed the door. He looked at the work piled on his desk—three living-will documents to finish drafting, two purchase contracts to review, and several other detailed tasks almost as exciting as those.

He sighed. Was this why he'd gone into law?

# 6

Nigel got to the Old Bailey on time the next morning, but there was a delay in getting into the courtroom itself. There were competing legal priorities, and they posed an architectural dilemma. On the one hand, the trial was public—like any trial in the Crown Courts criminal justice system. That was mandatory.

On the other hand, this jury had to remain anonymous.

There were seats in the main area of the courtroom, behind the lawyer's tables, available for family of the defendant and for the press. But there was also a gallery for the general public—essentially a balcony, overlooking the entire courtroom. A screen had to be set up that shielded the jury from both those views, but still allowed the jurors to see the defendant, the judge, the witnesses, and the lawyers, unimpeded.

Nigel waited in the corridor for Court 13, along with his fellow jurors and alternates. The group atmosphere was different now than during the jury selection. The urgent suspense of getting selected or not selected had been replaced with a more subdued sense of expectancy for what might come next.

Nigel saw the young woman with the tattoo, but was unable to talk to her. She was on her mobile the whole time.

The steward opened the courtroom door and called them in. The lawyers were at their places in the center front of the courtroom, with papers and binders stacked at their tables. But there were no spectators yet.

Ms. Sreenivasan guided the jurors to their seats, behind the eight-foot cloth screen, with a partial overhead awning that shielded the view from the gallery. After just a few moments, Mr. Walker told everyone to rise, the judge entered, and the court was called to order.

The judge invited Mr. Slattery to open for the prosecution. Slattery stood up from behind his table.

"Thank you, my lord," he said. And then he cleared his throat. He tucked in a lock of gray hair that had obstinately protruded below the back edge of his wig. He turned his head to look toward the jury. And then, catching sight of Nigel in the alternate jury section, Slattery remembered to look down and make sure that he had zipped his fly.

He had. All was in order. He put his hand on his chin and pretended to think for a moment.

Nigel wondered whether he was getting ready to waste the jury's time with gratuitous flattery in the opening statement. What Nigel personally needed, more than flattery, was a beverage. A water. Or, better, another coffee. Just thinking about that made him want to clear his throat.

Slattery approached the jury box, still apparently deep

in thought. Then he raised his head and began. "It is a difficult thing to lose our heroes," he said.

Good move, thought Nigel. Get right to it. And now Nigel did clear his throat. Quite unintentionally.

Slattery may have heard it, but if he did, he showed no obvious reaction.

Sorry about that, thought Nigel. But nice opening.

"It is a difficult thing to lose our heroes," said Slattery again. "We don't want to see them fall. Oh, the tabloids might enjoy it well enough, just to capture our ten pence, but we don't enjoy it, not really. We want our heroes to remain worthy of our admiration. And though we know that success in their athletic endeavors must someday yield to the ravages of time, we don't want to see that happen to their character. We don't want to see that at all, and we quite understandably resent it when anyone tries to insist that we do so.

"But you know and I know that we are all human. We are all fallible. And we all must be held accountable when our failures—our willful, intentional wrongs—do harm to another. That is justice. That is what our legal system is about.

"And I will ask you to remember that, as I describe for you the events that have brought us here today."

He paused. He was about to turn and look back at the defendant in a deliberately timed move for the jury.

Don't do it, thought Nigel. Not yet, not with this defendant. Everyone still loves him. Prove he's not a hero first, before you look at him.

But no—Slattery did it—he looked.

Nigel, almost subconsciously, shook his head and made a short note in his notebook.

The jurors, following the prosecutor's lead, were all now looking at McSweeney.

McSweeney—perhaps nudged by his own lawyers, Nigel was watching for it, but couldn't quite tell—looked back at the prosecutor, and then at the jurors—with a calm, reproachful expression that fairly reeked of innocence.

"Aww," said a juror in the back row of the main section, very softly, as though about to pat a puppy.

Slattery obviously heard it; he turned and put himself between the jurors and their view of the defendant.

"We shall," he said loudly, "through both forensic evidence and witness testimony, show that the defendant killed his own wife, from a motive as old as mankind, and as reprehensible and deserving of punishment now as it has ever been. He killed her because he thought he owned her. He killed her because he learned he could no longer possess her. And he killed her because he thought he was so much above the law that he could murder his own wife in a brutal, bloody, jealous rage—and get away with it."

Slattery paused just long enough to let the jurors form that image in their minds. Then he said, "In our society, no man is allowed to do that. Not even the greatest cricket player in the world."

Nice touch, thought Nigel, writing in his notebook. Negate his hero status. Maybe we won't think that it's contradictory to claim jealous rage and an expectation of getting away with it at the same time. And now see if you can make us love the victim more than the perpetrator.

Slattery continued. "We will begin on the date of August fifteenth. Exactly one week prior to Marlie McSweeney's death. In some ways, it was a day like any other for Marlie. But in another way, a very important way, it was not.

"On that morning, Marlie McSweeney met her friend Carole Stoddard for brunch at the Chelsea Rose Cafe. They both had lemon crepes—which they had enjoyed many times there before. This was the last lemon crepe, though, for Marlie."

Nigel made an entry in his notebook: Good tactic to reduce the meaning of life to a single dessert? A bit overdramatic for a lemon crepe? What if the jurors don't like French pastries?

"Carole will testify to what her friend Marlie told her over the lemon crepes and tea. About the state of their marriage."

Hearsay, thought Nigel. You won't get it in.

"And she will testify to what Marlie showed her before they left the café that morning."

Fair enough. That much you might get in. Second-hand show-and-tell won't work. But second-hand show by itself might, if all you want is what the witness saw with her own eyes.

"Later that afternoon, Marlie McSweeney went to the Sainsbury's grocery on Kings Road. She bought red potatoes, and reduced-calorie butter, and paper towels, and soap, and other sundries, just as you and I would, and . . ."

Nigel sighed—but only inwardly and silently—and he made another note: Right, you're humanizing the victim. But grocery lists are boring. And you still haven't told us *why* the defendant was in a jealous rage.

Slattery stopped in midsentence—turned away from the jury—thought about it for a moment—and then turned to the judge. "Really, my lord, I must object!"

The judge looked surprised. He motioned Slattery to come forward to the bench, and then whispered, "Object to what, Mr. Slattery? You are the only one who has been speaking."

"One of the alternate jurors is making notes about my opening statement!"

The judge puzzled over that for a moment. He looked toward the jury.

In the jury section, Nigel and all the others could see that a conversation was taking place, but they could not make out what was being said.

Perhaps this is some sort of strategic pause by the prosecutor, thought Nigel. A feint, before he thrusts home with the motive.

Nigel made a note of that.

The judge gave a quick, hard glance in Nigel's direction, and then he motioned the defense barrister to come to the bench and join the prosecutor. When Slattery and Langdon were both in place, the judge kept his voice low and said, "This is in fact the reason we give notebooks to jurors, is it not? So that they can take notes about the case for their eventual deliberations?"

"Yes, my lord," said the prosecutor, "but alternate juror number five is not so much taking notes about the case as he is making criticisms on my handling of it!"

"How do you know this, Mr. Slattery?"

"I can tell by his facial expressions."

"That's quite some ability my learned friend has," said Langdon, the defense barrister, with some amusement, "to read jurors' minds from their expressions like that."

"You won't like it if he does it when you're up," responded Slattery.

"Enough," said the judge. "Whether he's making such notes or not is moot, for two reasons. First, we all know that jurors talk about all of us—prosecution, defense, and judge—quite apart from the case itself. They shouldn't do it, we don't want them to do it, it's irrelevant to the case and to justice—but they do it anyway. We can only pray that they set all that aside when it comes to deliberations. And secondly—well, quite frankly, I'm pleased when I learn that jurors have taken a note or two, though not so many that they forget to listen and think. We know that many of them use their notebooks simply for doodling. I've heard of instances of jurors filling their notebooks with nothing but sketches of male and female naughty bits. Fortunately, the only time anyone looks at those—the notebooks, I mean—is when there is an allegation of some form of juror misconduct. There is no such allegation here, is there?"

"No," said the prosecutor.

"Of course not," said the defense.

"Let's resume, then, shall we?"

"Thank you, my lord," said Slattery, loud enough for the

jury to hear, so that they might think he had won the point, though he had lost it. "I have only one more thing to say."

He approached the jury. "Why was the defendant in a jealous rage? Why would a man in a marriage such as his, where his own philandering was winked at—"

I'd object to that, thought Nigel.

The defense did. "Objection, my lord," said Langdon. "The defendant is not on trial for infidelity and this is simple character assassination."

"Sustained. For the moment."

"I apologize, my lord," said Slattery quickly, having surely expected the objection. Then he turned to the jury and began again.

The defense barrister did not watch the prosecutor during this. Langdon pretended an interest in the alignment of his own wig, and the condition of his own fingernails, or any body part he was willing to focus on in public.

You're not fooling anyone, thought Nigel. You're listening as though your career depends on it.

"Why was the defendant in a jealous rage, you ask?" said Slattery again. "Simple. Because he had learned that his wife had done, in her own way, in her own consistent, hopeful, and needful way, what he had done to her repeatedly, thoughtlessly, and arrogantly for the length of their marriage. She had been untrue. She had taken a lover."

Langdon was now listening so intently while pretending not to that he accidentally created a hangnail on his left hand.

"Who was this lover, you might ask. My learned friend opposing counsel will most certainly ask—you can see that he is waiting anxiously right now to see if we will promise more than we can deliver. The defense knows what we know—which is that, despite all our best efforts, we have not been able to identify the lover to whom Marlie McSweeney wrote her letters. That is true. But I submit to you that the identity of the lover does not matter. All that matters is that there was a mechanism by which Liam McSweeney learned of that lover's existence. And that we will show."

Slattery paused for a deep and (he hoped) profound sigh, and then he continued.

"Liam McSweeney heard rumors of an affair, heard rumors of letters—and believed that his wife had found someone who fulfilled all her needs in ways that he himself did not even try to do, and he murdered her out of the most ancient of motives . . . out of jealousy. Selfish . . . grasping . . . jealousy."

Slattery stopped, nodded to the judge slightly to show that he was done, and then stood very still.

Nigel looked toward the defense barrister. Langdon was no longer looking at his fingernails. The man's wall of feigned indifference had been broken. He was not happy. The inability of the prosecution to identify any individual alleged to be Marlie McSweeney's lover was a major hole in the theory that Liam McSweeney had killed her in a jealous rage. But now Slattery had inoculated the jury against that flaw. True, the prosecution didn't have the identity of the lover. But they didn't need it. All they had to show was that Liam McSweeney learned of an affair. And for that, they had the letters.

Might have done it only a little better myself, thought Nigel.

The prosecution had completed its opening statement; there would not be a defense opening statement—it was an English trial, and the prosecution would simply begin to present its case, and the defense would begin to poke new holes in it. Or try to.

So much more fun to be the defense, thought Nigel. Provided that you think your client might be innocent—and that if you do believe it, you win it.

"Are you ready with your first witness?" said the judge to the prosecution.

"We certainly are, my lord," said Slattery.

The judge looked at the wall clock. "Given the hour, do you want to proceed now, or break for lunch first?"

You should let us break now, thought Nigel. We'll go to lunch with your statement fresh in our minds. But if you just charge ahead and we get to the canteen late, we'll blame it on you.

"I know the jury must be very hungry," said Slattery, "and I hear there's an excellent pasta today. I'm happy to wait until after lunch."

"We'll break then," said the judge. "But I suggest you not make promises about the canteen pasta."

The judge was about to rise—but a hand shot up from the alternates section. And when no one acknowledged it immediately, the hand waved back and forth as eagerly as if hailing a cab.

Everyone looked.

It was the tall alternate juror.

Ms. Sreenivasan, expecting some sort of personal emergency, quickly went to him and whispered, "Yes?"

"I have several questions for the prosecution," said the tall man, not whispering. "First, do the McSweeneys employ a housekeeping service? And secondly, regarding finger-prints—"

"Jurors do not ask questions during opening statements," said the judge, quickly and sternly.

"But several salient points have been overlooked."

"It is not up to you," said the judge quickly, "to try to improve upon the prosecution's opening statement. Further, remember that the statement is not evidence itself, but merely a preview of what the prosecution hopes to show. When testimony is presented, you will have the opportunity to submit, in writing, specific questions for specific witnesses, subject to my approval."

"Oh."

"Is that clear?"

"Yes. But just one thing—are we to apply the general principle that when the impossible has been eliminated, whatever remains, however improbable, must be the truth?"

The judge drummed his fingers on the bench, like someone doing a five-finger piano sequence, and stared hard and suspiciously at the tall juror.

"What you just stated is not a principle of law," said the judge. "I will give you the applicable law, and the criteria by which you must apply it, at the end of the trial, before the jury begins deliberations—assuming we come to that. In the meantime, your job is to simply pay attention to the evidence presented to you. Jurors do not make remarks upon the case in open court. Do you understand?"

"Yes."

"Thank you so very much."

Now the judge turned to the rest of the jury. "I think this is a good time to take a break. Remember all my admonitions. Do not discuss this case with anyone. Not the general public. Not your family members. And above all not the press. Some of you may feel an impulse as you walk into the corridor to whip out your mobile phones and call your BFFs, or whatever the term is that my granddaughter uses, and tell them what case you are on. Do not do so. Don't make me take your phones away. You may say that you are on a jury, but you are forbidden to say which one. You may say what time you expect to be home for supper, but you may not talk about this case when you get there. Remember that you are an anonymous jury, and we intend to keep it that way. The alternative would be sequestration, and I'm sure no one wants that."

He paused now, trying to look sternly at all the jurors at once.

"Is that clear? If it is not, now is the time to speak."

No one spoke. The judge waited until he saw two or three affirmative nods. "Very well, then. Please return to the corridor no later than five minutes before the hour; you will wait there for Ms. Sreenivasan to call you in. Court will resume promptly at two p.m. Not ten minutes past. Not five minutes past. Two p.m. promptly. Do not inconvenience this court and your fellow jurors by being late. Thank you. We will now go on break. The canteen service queue shuts down at half past one. Proceed accordingly."

## 7

The McSweeney courtroom was not the only one breaking for lunch. Most of the others were as well, and experienced jurors from all the courtrooms, knowing the gravity of their situation, were rushing madly to get to the canteen before it could close and leave them nothing to eat but machine-vended Mars bars.

The gleaming wood stairwell (just polished the night before, the Crown Court maintenance division wanting its best foot forward for such a celebrated trial) that descended from the courtroom level to the canteen was normally wide enough to accommodate any traffic it might receive.

Not today, with so many courts in session and so many famished jurors in a desperate hurry. They did not actually run down the stairs (being English, after all), or at least they pretended not to—but Nigel noticed most of them trying to proceed at an abnormally fast walk. There were more than a few jostles and apologies, and even a few non-apologies, by the time they reached the relative safety of the lower floor.

When Nigel finally reached the food queue itself, it was already more than fifty jurors deep. Nigel sighed, took his place in line, and told his stomach to stop growling. The queue grew longer, and the corridor more crowded, with jurors and others trying to hustle through in both directions. At one point the entire line had to shift left, flat up against the corridor wall, as two officials, one of them carrying a first-aid kit, pushed their way through, heading in the direction of the courtroom stairwell. The crowd was much too thick to see what the issue was.

In the meantime, the line continued to inch forward. In ten more minutes, Nigel finally got close enough to pick up his food tray, and someone put a hand on his arm. Nigel turned. It was the woman with the tattoo.

"I'm Lucy. Will you sit at a table with me and shield me from one of the other jurors?"

Nigel processed that quickly. "Done. I'm Nigel. Which juror?"

She looked around. "I don't see him yet. I'll let you know. Do you know anything about the food here?"

"Avoid the shepherd's pie, if they offer it. I hear they include elements of the shepherd. And shepherds aren't as cleanly as one might hope."

"They said something about a pasta?"

"Yes," said Nigel, "but get the red sauce, not the white."

They both did that. They took their trays out into the common eating area and sat at one of the large Formica tables.

"There he is now," said Lucy. "That's him."

Nigel looked. Just now coming through the cashier queue

was the tall man who Nigel had spoken to earlier in the alley. The one who had interrupted the opening statements. He had a pad of paper out, and he was jotting something down as the cashier rang up his lunch.

"Him?"

"Yes," she said. "He smells like pipe smoke. He ran to catch up with me on the stairs, and he keeps trying to talk to me for some reason. And he says he has lots of questions for the judge. See, there he is, writing them out right now. Is he allowed to do that?"

"He shouldn't be writing notes except in the courtroom, and he has to leave them there on our breaks. Perhaps he's writing something else. But yes, when opening arguments are completed and we get to the witness testimony, the judge can allow questions. And I expect there will be some."

"When he followed me in the stairway, he was talking about how he's going to want to see the witnesses' hands, and their hats, and their shoes, and their watch fobs."

"Watch fobs?"

"Yes. I don't think I've ever seen a real-life watch fob. Have you?"

"Not since my great-grandfather died."

"And he keeps staring at me."

"Yes. Well. Regarding staring—"

"I mean in a weird way."

"Just for my own future reference, how do you distinguish between staring in a weird way and staring—"

"Omigod, he's coming over. Don't look!"

And yes, indeed, the tall alternate juror was coming over.

"I said not to look!" said Lucy.

"Well," said Nigel, who had looked, "you should have said that first, and then said that he was coming over. I can take instructions, but they need to be in the proper order."

Now the man was only a few feet from their table. And now he was right next to them.

And now he kept walking, with his tray, right on by.

"Oh," said Lucy.

"Disappointed?" said Nigel.

"I'll bet he was coming to our table, but then you looked, and so he didn't."

"Yes," said Nigel. "I sometimes have that effect on people."

Then suddenly, at the last moment, just as they were settling in, the tall man turned and came back to join them.

"What did you two get?" he said, pulling up a chair.

As he put his tray down on the table, other jurors from the lunch queue, seeing a group begin to form, brought their trays over as well.

"I got fish-and-chips," said the tall man. "Hope they have the same next week. I mean, if it goes that long. Do you think it will?"

The pensioner widow and the man with the calloused hands sat down at the table now. They introduced themselves as Armstrong and Mrs. Peabody.

"I don't think we're supposed to talk about the trial, are we?" said Mrs. Peabody.

"No," said Nigel, trying to hide his disappointment at the arrival of a crowd. "We're not."

"A technicality," said the man with the expensive shoes, who joined them now. "Everyone does talk." He introduced himself as Bankstone, and he took the chair on the other side of Lucy.

"I wish we weren't on a murder case though," said Lucy. "I had a friend who was on a brutal rape case—they detailed each of the several counts, and everything that led up to them. When she went home at night, she wanted to tell her husband about it, but you're not allowed to talk about the case. She had to go in for counseling after."

"If it's graphic medical testimony you're concerned about," said Mrs. Peabody, "I was on a civil case involving a malfunctioning wood chipper that was as awful as anything you can imagine."

"But the stakes are so high," said Lucy. "What if we get the verdict wrong?"

"The police and the lawyers and the judge have to do their jobs first," said Nigel. "Then we decide based on what they present to us."

"Yes, but if the lawyers say it's really up to the jury, and we say it's really up to the lawyers, then who is really responsible?"

"It's just like raising children to adulthood, dear," said Mrs. Peabody. "There are some things that are up to you—and there are some other things that just aren't, no matter how sad they might make you."

"Even so," said Lucy. "I'm glad I'm an alternate and not one of the regular jurors. I don't want to have to decide someone's fate."

"You won't be doing it by yourself, dear," said Mrs. Peabody. "We'll all do it together. It is rather tricky, I admit—you have to be independent enough to have your own point of view, and cooperative enough to listen to everyone else's. In every one of the juries I've been on, we reached a verdict. Either there never was any real doubt—or else there was plenty of it—and we all felt the same way. Perhaps we were just lucky, though."

"I saw one fellow get dismissed from the jury pool because he said he wouldn't convict no matter what the evidence showed," said Armstrong. "He said he thought everyone is entitled to one mistake."

"That's what he said, but it's not what he meant," said Nigel. "What he meant was that he wouldn't convict because he was willing to give his hero a pass."

"True," nodded the tall juror.

"Don't either of you believe in second chances?" said Mrs. Peabody.

The tall juror raised an eyebrow at that, but didn't answer immediately. He took a moment to douse his fish-and-chips generously with vinegar and inhale the scent of it striking the still-hot deep-fried batter. Then he said, "I very much believe in second chances. But that doesn't mean you don't pay a price. You make your one mistake, and then you are lucky or unlucky in the consequences of it, and then you recover from it as best you are able, and then you repeat the process. With new mistakes. And with some correct choices as well, probably, but of course it's not always easy to tell one from the other."

"So we're talking about life here, or the law?" said Nigel.

"Oh, sorry," said the tall juror, and then he bit into the flaky white fish with obvious satisfaction. "In my opinion, the food here is better than its reputation."

Nigel took that remark as an invitation to talk about something else, but Mrs. Peabody wasn't willing to let it go quite yet.

"How did you know that the man in the back row would get dismissed?"

"Simple," said the tall juror. "It was warm in the courtroom, and everyone else had removed their macs and sweaters. But not him. He kept his mac on, zipped up to the neck. Now, this could have been either because he was wearing a McSweeney cricket jersey underneath, or because he had an England cricket team tattoo on his neck or forearms, but because he was actually sweating from too much clothing, I concluded it was a jersey that he was trying to conceal. He wore it to the courthouse to proclaim his support for McSweeney, but he covered it up with his jacket when it looked like he had a chance of getting on the jury. It was obvious and I knew the judge would dismiss him."

"That's a lot from a zipped jacket," said Mrs. Peabody.

"No," said the tall juror, "not within the context. You can tell quite a lot about anyone from their appearance, and that information is amplified exponentially if you know just the slightest bit of their current or past circumstances."

"For example?" said Bankstone.

The tall juror put down his fork and glanced at all four of the alternate jurors seated around him.

First he looked at Nigel and at Lucy.

"No, I don't think I should do yours at the moment," he said to Nigel. "Or yours," he said to Lucy.

"Well, if you don't do someone, we're not going to believe you," said Mrs. Peabody. "Try me. I should be easy."

"You married at a young age, remained so for more than forty years, until your husband passed away. He was in the legal profession himself, probably a judge. You miss him."

She raised an eyebrow, pondered for a moment, then said, "You got most of that because I moved my wedding ring, along with my ruby anniversary band, to my right hand."

"Yes. Easy, as you said."

"But how do you know my late husband was a judge?"

"You said in court that you've done jury duty three times, all in the last six years. Something prevented you from being eligible before that. Until very recently, officers of the court were absolutely prohibited in England from being on jury service, and their spouses typically would not be impaneled, either. So you did not begin to be placed on juries until after he passed away. The expensive design of the clothes you are wearing suggests that he was a judge, as opposed to some lower officer of the court."

"Fair enough," said Mrs. Peabody. "Now do someone else."

"How about him?" said Lucy.

She was indicating Bankstone, the man with the expensive haircut, and the expensive casual clothes, and the very expensive shoes. A man who was taller than Nigel, in better shape than Nigel, and clearly making much more money.

Nigel found her apparent interest discouraging.

"Do you mind?" she said to the man, leaning toward him a bit.

"No, go right ahead," he said, smiling slightly.

"Investment broker," said the tall juror. "Partly from your

haircut, but mostly from your shoes. You tried to get excused because of a planned vacation, but you've used that excuse once before already this year, so they kept you on over your objection."

"That's close," said the man, quite enthusiastically. "I was a derivatives day trader, but now I'm in biomedical/pharmaceutical acquisitions."

"What's that?" said Nigel.

"Surprisingly simple. I buy a small biomed company that isn't doing well but still has some drugs that are under patent, or even generic drugs for which it is the only manufacturer. Then I cut back on the resources that are dead weight—that is to say, the research division—and then I raise the price on the patented or unique drugs as high as the market will bear—and then, having made all those improvements, I sell the whole thing to the highest bidder and move on to my next project."

Lucy took perhaps two seconds to absorb that information—and then she very subtly edged away from him at the table.

I still have a shot, thought Nigel.

"Now him," said Lucy, indicating Nigel.

"Barrister," said the tall man. "They almost threw you out, but they were so desperate to fill the quota that they kept you on."

"Wrong," said Nigel. "Not a barrister. Only a solicitor."

The tall man studied Nigel for a moment. "My error. It was a close call, I should have said simply 'lawyer,' to cover both possibilities. It's a capital mistake to theorize before one has all the facts."

Nigel recognized that phrase immediately. He knew where he had read it—many times. But he had never heard anyone say it in real life.

"You've evaluated our occupations," said Nigel. "What about yours?"

"I'm a musician," said the tall juror. "You may call me Siger. The longer form is Sigerson, but that's been overused."

Now the steward stepped in at the canteen entrance. "Your attention please. All jurors from court number thirteen, please return to the courtroom immediately."

There were murmurs and a commotion of eating utensils, and everyone in the canteen looked questioningly toward the steward. "Again, jurors from court thirteen. Jurors from court thirteen only. Both primary jurors and alternates. Please return immediately to the courtroom. You may bring your portable food items with you, this one time only. Thank you."

Nigel and Lucy both stood, and she started to pick up her plate of unfinished pasta.

"I wouldn't," said Nigel. "Portable means a bag of crisps. And you don't want to be sitting there for three hours with that plate in your lap."

In Court 13, the judge was already in place as the summoned jurors filed in. But the door to his chambers was ajar. He was leaning his chin on his hand, his elbow on the bench, staring down at a document, and he did not look happy.

Ms. Sreenivasan motioned for the jurors to take their seats, and then she closed the courtroom doors. The judge looked over at the jurors. "I'm sorry to interrupt your lunch," he said.

The scent of fish-and-chips with vinegar filled the room. The judge inhaled. "And I myself am so very, very hungry. However, I have some sad news. You may have noticed that there is one empty seat among you. This morning there were twelve of you seated as primary jurors, and now there are eleven."

Everyone looked at the primary jury section—except the people in the spectator and press galleries, who couldn't see around the partition, and so had to content themselves with murmuring. And except the barristers for both defense and prosecution, who wanted to pretend (at least to the jury itself) that exactly who was a juror and who not was a matter of complete indifference to them.

"It is always sad when we lose one of our own. I regret to tell you that less than an hour ago, when we broke for lunch"—the judge paused now, wincing at his own choice of words, but then had no choice but to just continue—"juror number seven, in the process of descending the stairs to the canteen, slipped and fell. Fortunately, her knitting needles were carefully stowed, and so no one else was injured—but she herself has broken her hip."

There were gasps in the courtroom—not just from the jurors, but from the public galleries as well.

The judge hastily added, "Please do not be alarmed. She is already in hospital, X-rays have been taken, and there is no reason not to expect a full recovery. I know that you will all be anxious to extend your kind sympathies and well-wishes, which you cannot do because of our necessary anonymity—but rest assured that the court shall do so for you. But now—to the issue at hand. One alternate juror must now take the place of primary juror seven, so that we will have the requisite dozen. Jury selection for this trial has concluded, and so we cannot add another to the alternate pool—but fortunately we had the foresight to begin with five alternates, and certainly that will last us through the duration. Most certainly it will."

Now the judge looked directly at the five jurors in the alternates section.

His stare seemed full of portent, and the suspense among the alternates was palpable. The order in which the alternates would be used as replacements had been determined randomly, without regard to the order in which they had initially been selected. The alternates looked at each other and then at the judge, wondering who would become the replacement primary juror. The judge and Mr. Walker and Ms. Sreenivasan all consulted their list—and then the judge looked up.

"Alternate juror number two—please take the empty seat in the primary section. You are now primary juror number seven."

Lucy sighed in relief. So did Bankstone. Siger looked, if anything, a bit disappointed.

Mrs. Peabody stood and willingly went into the primary section and sat in the empty seat.

"Thank you," said the judge. Then he looked at another memo he had before him. After a moment's study he looked out at the entire courtroom.

"I mentioned earlier that to protect your anonymity and the judicial process, we might need to take some extraordinary measures regarding the press," he began. He cast an accusing glance at the area where the media was seated.

"This screen that shields our jurors from the prying eyes and pressure of the media is one of those measures. It is necessary but not sufficient, and I have decided to take some additional steps."

The judge turned and addressed the jurors. "For every day of this trial, for its entire duration, the court has decided to provide private transportation for each of you, to your homes, or places of business, or the tube, or wherever you choose—in a way that will ensure your anonymity when you leave the courthouse and keep the hounds of the press off your backs. We will begin doing that today; the steward will escort you to the transportation. Also, because of the unfortunate accident in the stairwell this morning, I have decided that we have put you through enough stress for one day, and we will adjourn early."

The judge turned and looked out at the broader courtroom. "Members of the press and public, you will kindly remain seated in the galleries until after the jurors have departed the courtroom and the stewards have opened the doors for you."

And then back to the jury. "Court is adjourned. Remember all my admonitions, and I will see you all back here promptly tomorrow morning at ten thirty a.m."

## 8

Have you heard the latest about Liam McSweeney?"

"Probably not," said Nigel. "But no need to tell me."

Hendricks apparently didn't hear that response. He had *The Daily Sun* open, and he proceeded to read from it.

" 'The chairman of the England and Wales Cricket Board has announced that after a meeting of the full board and consultation with the Discipline Standing Committee, it has been decided that Liam McSweeney *will* play in the opening match, unless convicted of the charges currently pending in Crown Court. The chairman stated in his announcement that Mr. McSweeney has pled his complete innocence and asserted a defense. And to deprive a man of his livelihood before he has had his day in court would violate the very standards of fair play that make cricket and England what they are today. Shortly after the chairman's remarks, the odds in favor of an English victory in the first match improved from even to two to one.' "

"How about that?" said Hendricks, slapping the paper on his desk. "I knew they'd come round to it!"

"And you were right, of course," said Nigel. "But a small favor—when I sign in over the next few weeks, avoid reading the paper to me if you can?"

This time Hendricks was palpably offended. He started to get up from the chair, nearly shaking with umbrage.

"Well then, Mr. Heath, if you don't want me to share the news with you, then—"

And then he stopped.

"Say—how's that jury thing going?" he said. "Are you on one?"

"Can't talk about it," said Nigel.

A lightbulb went on for Hendricks. "Aha! So that's—mum's the word, Heath, mum's the word!"

"I've never liked cricket anyway," said Nigel, heading for the lift. "When I want a game that can go on forever and whose rules are incomprehensible to the layman, I prefer the law."

That evening, Nigel sat in his office at Baker Street Chambers, tried to focus on his day job, and wondered if perhaps he should have chosen a different specialty of law.

Her Majesty's Courts Service paid jurors a stipend for each day of service. But if you were self-employed, as Nigel was, you still had to keep your clients happy.

And he was having trouble focusing. He would have preferred to be at the corner pub—but the corner pub was a sports bar, with multiple tellys tuned to the sporting news, and many inebriated cricket fans, and it would have been impossible to go there and not run into all sorts of information sources and speculation that he was supposed to be avoiding.

So he stayed in his office. But his mind kept turning back to the trial—partly to the details of it, but even more to the tactics of the opposing barristers.

He was pretty sure he could do a better job.

And when he tried to think of something else, what popped into his mind was not the estate document he was supposed to be working on, with all its obscure prose and provisions, but the glimpse of a rose tattoo—or a heart or a butterfly, whatever it might be—on Lucy's freckled skin in a half-concealed location.

## 9

The following week, each afternoon when the court adjourned, a fleet of unmarked sedans, in different styles from one day to the next, waited in the Lewes Street alley. The street was blocked, the jurors were hustled into the vehicles, two jurors for each car, and then they were driven home by professionals who knew how to lose the salivating media.

All of which would have been fine with Nigel, if Lucy had been in his car.

But she wasn't. Apparently their respective destinations in London were geographically incompatible. And it was never possible to talk to her alone at the lunch break. So the only real opportunity for conversation was while walking down the stairs from the courtroom to the exit, which didn't work, because she was always in a hurry for some reason.

And so even though Nigel was perfectly willing to ignore the judge's injunction against fraternizing, no fraternization was taking place anyway.

There was nothing to do but focus on the trial.

The first witness to take the stand was Chief Inspector Wembley. All eyes followed him as he took his place in the box.

Or, at least, most eyes did. Of the twelve primary jurors, the only one who did not seem to be paying close attention was the annoyed Bankstone. Nigel and the alternates were, if anything, more attentive than the primary jurors—like junior varsity hoping to move up to the main team. Siger, in particular, leaned forward, hunching his narrow shoulders in concentration.

As Wembley was sworn in, Siger nudged Lucy with his elbow. "Notice the heavyset shoulders," he whispered, though loudly. "Rounded a bit now with middle age, but he clearly played sports back in the day. Rugby though, not cricket— your typical police officer comes from a background that can't afford the pricier sports—and this one is no exception to the rule, judging from his worn dress shoes—on an occasion when he surely is wearing the best that he has."

Lucy, trying not to encourage him, only nodded slightly and said nothing.

"Shhh," said Mrs. Peabody, leaning toward them.

And now the judge looked over.

"Is there something you would like to share with us all . . . alternate juror one?" said the judge, and the bailiff reinforced it by glowering.

"No," said Siger. "I apologize, my lord."

The judge nodded quickly and dismissively, and told the prosecuting attorney to proceed.

Mr. Slattery began by asking Chief Inspector Wembley to describe the crime scene at McSweeney's home—but then stopped him.

"Sorry, one moment, chief inspector—my lord, I had hoped that we might mention first to the jury that counseling will be available for them, should they find these rather graphic details and accompanying photos upsetting—"

"Objection, my lord!" Langdon was on his feet. "The jurors know full well about the available counseling, and my learned friend is bringing it up now only for the purpose of telling them how they should feel about what they are about to see!"

"Yes, a fair point," said the judge. "The counseling is mentioned in our brochures, after all."

He turned toward the jury. "The jury will disregard— well, the jury will not disregard that the counseling is available—but will disregard the apparent attempt by the prosecution to tell them what to feel about testimony still to be presented." And then back to the lawyers, "There, I think that covers it. Now, please let us proceed."

Slattery continued with his questions, letting Wembley walk the jurors mentally through the crime scene, and previewing the photo exhibits that would come from the forensics team's testimony.

And then, when asked to describe the blood on the cricket bat, Wembley paused.

Most of the jury probably thought this was because of the gore, but Nigel knew Wembley better than that. He was too seasoned to falter at the notion of blood on a weapon. What gave Wembley pause was that he simply couldn't bear to say what he was going to have to say next. He was too much of a sports fan for that—whether or not he played cricket himself.

"Is there anything special about that particular cricket bat?" said the prosecutor.

Wembley took a deep breath, and the defense attorney took advantage of the pause to jump in.

"Objection, my lord," said Langdon. "The witness is not an expert on cricket bats."

Mistake, thought Nigel. The witness is already reluctant. By challenging him, you just make his testimony more convincing.

"I'll rephrase," said Slattery, quickly. "Inspector Wembley, does this particular cricket bat have any identifying marks on it that might cause you, even with your limited knowledge of cricket bats, to form an opinion as to whom the bat might belong?"

"Objection—"

"Please," said the judge. "Anyone with even modest knowledge of cricket will know what those marks are. Let's save some time and allow this witness to state it. If you think there is any expert who will challenge his testimony, you will have your opportunity later."

Wembley proceeded with his answer. "The bat has three international cricket championship emblems on it, with the England team as champions, for each of those years. There is only one player in England who was on each of those teams."

"And who is that?" said the prosecutor.

"Liam McSweeney." Inspector Wembley sighed; he seemed on the verge of tears over it.

"Did the Scotland Yard forensics lab perform tests on this bat?"

"Yes. It was tested for blood. And for fingerprints."

"What did the blood test show?"

"The blood on the bat was Marlie McSweeney's. No other blood was found."

"Did this bat—this bat with Marlie McSweeney's blood on it—have any fingerprints on it?"

"Yes. The tests showed Liam McSweeney's fingerprints."

Of course it did, thought Nigel. It was his own cricket bat.

"Did the tests show anyone else's prints?"

"No," said Wembley. "The only prints found on the bat were from Liam McSweeney."

"Thank you," said the prosecutor. "Nothing further."

Langdon, Q.C., stood up for the defense. He approached Wembley with an expression that could only be described as a sympathetic smile.

"Do you follow the sport of cricket fairly closely, Inspector Wembley?" said the defense barrister.

"As much as the next man," said Wembley. "Perhaps a little more."

"In your opinion, is it within Liam McSweeney's character to have committed this crime?"

"Objection," said Slattery. "The inspector surely cannot speculate as to—"

"Sustained," said the judge. "You know better, Mr. Langdon."

"I apologize, my lord. Inspector, does it surprise you that the bat that Liam McSweeney used in three championship games would have his fingerprints on it?"

"No."

"Nothing further, my lord," said Langdon.

"Redirect?" said the judge to the prosecution.

"No, my lord," said Slattery.

Wembley started to get up from the witness box, and the judge was about to officially excuse him, and the barristers for both sides were getting ready to move on—when they all caught sight of sudden motion within the alternate jury section.

Siger was standing, and waving his arms as if a bus was about to pass him by. And as soon as the judge and barristers looked in his direction, he spoke. "Do the McSweeneys employ a cleaning service at the house?" he said, quite loudly.

"Alternate juror one, if you continue these interruptions, I might have to hold you in contempt."

"Oh. I am sorry, my lord. I thought that we would be allowed to ask questions, and so—"

"My fault, I'm sure, for not being more explicit," said the judge. "The process is this—after each witness, you may write questions on pages from your notebook. You will give those to Ms. Sreenivasan, and I will review them and decide whether they should be asked. Is that clear?"

"Yes."

"Good. Now then—are there any questions from the jury?"

Siger's hand shot up again. No one else's.

The judge sighed and nodded.

Ms. Sreenivasan collected a folded note from Siger and took it to the judge. The judge unfolded it, read it quickly, and then called both barristers forward to see it as well.

Both barristers read it—and then shrugged.

The judge nodded, sent them back to their places, and then turned again toward the jury. "Thank you for your note, alternate juror one, but your question regarding a cleaning service has no relevance for this witness. Are there any further questions from the jury?"

No one raised a hand.

"Excellent. The prosecution may call its next witness."

Slattery stood and called Sergeant Thackeray.

Langdon immediately stood as well. "We object to this witness, my lord. He can add nothing to the evidence that Inspector Wembley has already stated, and the defense is willing to stipulate to those facts. This witness is unnecessary and the prosecution is calling him only for the purpose of inflaming the jury."

Weak objection, thought Nigel. It will be denied.

And, indeed, Slattery had a quick response.

"My lord, Sergeant Thackeray was the first law enforcement officer on the scene. Surely his testimony is relevant."

"It certainly could be," said the judge. "The witness may take the stand."

Sergeant Thackeray took the stand. He looked even less happy about being there than Wembley was.

The prosecutor began. "Sergeant Thackeray, were you sent out on a call in Hampstead on the day in question?"

"Yes."

"Where was that call?"

"It was the . . . the McSweeney residence."

"What did you find when you got there?"

"I was met at the front of the residence by the gardener. He escorted me to the back of the residence."

"For what purpose?"

"To show me . . ." Sergeant Thackeray paused. He cleared his throat. "What he had found."

"And what was that?"

"The body of Mrs. Marlie McSweeney," he said, a bit hoarsely.

"And what condition was the body in?"

"Mrs. McSweeney was dead. Bludgeoned to death."

"Can you be more specific?"

Nigel could see the defense barrister half out of his seat, ready to object. But he didn't need to.

"I'm sure you can call the forensics examiner to give you the details," said Sergeant Thackeray to the prosecutor.

Langdon mulled it over, and then apparently decided to do just that.

"That's all right, Sergeant Thackeray. You needn't describe it."

The prosecution wants something else from this witness, thought Nigel. What is it?

Slattery started to turn away, as though he were done— clearly a feint—and then he turned back.

"Sergeant Thackeray, was this the first time you were called to the McSweeney residence?"

"Objection, my lord!" Langdon leaped from his seat as though he were on a coiled spring.

"Approach," said the judge.

Both barristers did so. They spoke with the judge in low whispers so that the jury couldn't hear. But Siger leaned forward, watching intently.

"The prosecution is trying to introduce evidence of an alleged prior bad act," said Langdon. "It is inflammatory and has no bearing on this case."

"It goes to both state of mind of the victim and the motive of the defendant," said Slattery.

"I want to hear it," said the judge. "If I change my mind after, I'll instruct the jury to ignore it."

"That will be bloody too late," muttered Langdon, so low that even the judge could barely hear it—but he did.

"It's the best you're going to get, counselor," said the judge. "Step back."

Slattery continued his questions. "Sergeant Thackeray, was this the first time you were called to the McSweeney residence?"

"No. I was called there once before."

"When?"

"Three years ago."

"For what reason?"

"A domestic disturbance call."

"Who placed the call?"

"Mrs. McSweeney."

"And what did Mrs. McSweeney tell you when you arrived at the scene?"

Langdon was on his feet again for the defense. This time, there was no whispering. "My lord, I strenuously object. Mrs. McSweeney is not available to be cross-examined. Whatever Sergeant Thackeray recalls from any possible conversation with her is hearsay."

Slattery displayed his most condescending smile. "That's true, she is not. We all know why. My lord, I withdraw that question. I will happily confine myself to what can be supported independently of Sergeant Thackeray's recollection."

"Then do so."

"Sergeant Thackeray—was the disturbance call itself recorded?"

"Yes. It is standard practice at our station to record all incoming calls."

"And do you have in front of you a transcript from that recording?"

"Yes."

The defense barrister looked as though he were considering another challenge.

Careful, thought Nigel. Technically, perhaps it's still hearsay. But better to hear the transcript than the victim's voice from beyond the grave. And if you point out that the transcript can't be cross-examined any more than the deceased can, you might open the testimony up to everything that Thackeray saw when he went on the call. You probably don't want that.

"Would you read it for us, please?" said the prosecutor.

"Which part?"

"Just the first line. What Mrs. McSweeney said first when the call was received."

The sergeant looked very carefully at the transcript in

front of him. Then he read it aloud, flatly and unemotionally. "'Mrs. McSweeney's voice: "Help me. He's hit me. He hit me. Please come at once."'"

"And then after that, she identifies herself and gives her address, correct?"

"Yes."

"Thank you. Nothing further."

The defense barrister stayed in his seat, hesitating.

There's only one thing you want to point out now, thought Nigel.

"Cross?" offered the judge.

"A bit, my lord," said Langdon, "but it's not the first time a ruling hasn't gone my way."

The judge almost smiled at that, but not quite, and he told Langdon to proceed. Langdon did so.

"Sergeant Thackeray, were any charges filed as a result of this call?"

"No."

"Thank you," said Langdon. "Just one more thing. Would you please read that exact transcript statement aloud again, please?

Sergeant Thackeray did so.

"Thank you. I believe I did not hear the defendant's name in that statement. I only heard the pronoun 'he.' Thank you, sergeant, no further questions."

"But when I arrived at their home, the only person there besides Mrs. McSweeney was her husband," said the sergeant quickly.

"Nonresponsive and move to strike!" said Langdon.

"My lord, I object to this tactic!" said Slattery. "If my learned friend has a question, he should ask it and allow the witness to answer. If instead he merely wants to express his own opinion about what he has heard, he can very well save it for his closing!"

"I suppose he can," said the judge. "Mr. Langdon, save your commentary. Mr. Slattery, do you feel a need to redirect?"

"No, my lord."

"The witness may step down."

The witness did so, and that was it. The witness did not look happy. The prosecutor did not look happy. The defense did not look happy. And Nigel was not satisfied as a juror with what he had heard in the testimony. But the judge showed only the annoyance of a man who had been through it all before, and the trial moved on.

Over the next week, the jurors heard testimony from Helen O'Shea, the forensics examiner, who brought details and photographs of the scene that Wembley had described only generally. The jurors heard testimony about shoe sizes and brands and unique tread patterns, about fingerprints on cricket bats, including when and how gloves were used in the game—and including that of a cleaning lady, called by the prosecution on the second day of testimony, who said that she was in the habit of dusting the trophy displays every week, including the cricket bat, which had hung prominently on the wall. As it happened, she had wiped it down only two days before it had been used on Mrs. McSweeney.

Siger seemed very gratified when that witness was called.

Nigel nodded to him politely, though it was not clear whether the prosecution had intended it all along or not.

Then came the day for the final prosecution witness. In Nigel's opinion, it would make or break the prosecution's case .

So far, all the witnesses called had provided only forensic testimony about the crime scene. It was bloody good forensic testimony, to be sure—but there had not been one word spoken about motive since the prosecution's opening statement.

Was proof of motive absolutely necessary? No. Would the judge make that clear in his instructions? Almost certainly. Would the jury follow those instructions to the letter and ignore what would seem to them a flaw in the case, when all of England was demanding an acquittal? That was not certain at all.

Besides, the prosecution had already promised a motive. They had bloody well better deliver it.

The prosecution called Carole Stoddard to the stand.

She was forty years of age, stylishly dressed, and tanned and fit in appearance.

Slattery began his questions and confirmed with the witness that she had joined Marlie McSweeney for brunch at the Chelsea Rose Cafe one week prior to the slaying. He asked her what they had talked about, and Langdon was on his feet immediately.

"Objection, my lord, anything this witness heard Mrs. McSweeney say, other than perhaps what she ordered for lunch, would surely be hearsay."

"My lord, certainly the witness can testify to the general

subject matter of a conversation in which she herself was a participant."

"I'll allow that as far as her own part in it," said the judge. "But proceed cautiously, Mr. Slattery."

Slattery turned back to the witness.

"What did you talk about?".

"The usual thing."

"Did the usual thing include personal relationships?"

"Yes."

Nigel glanced at Langdon, who was coiled like a spring.

"And did you say anything to Mrs. McSweeney about the state of your own personal relationships?"

"Relevance!" cried Langdon.

The judge waved that one off, and the witness answered. "I told her about an affair I was having."

"My lord . . ."

"And did she say anything in response?"

"She said she was having one, too."

The defense lawyer fairly flew out of his chair. "My lord, this is hearsay!"

This will be fun, thought Nigel. Another twist in the law student's Rubik's Cube.

The prosecution was ready for it. "My lord, it is an exception to the hearsay rule. It is a declaration against interest on the part of Mrs. McSweeney."

Wrong approach, thought Nigel.

"That exception seems a little thin here, Mr. Slattery," said the judge. "It's not as though she was admitting to a crime."

Slattery tried another tack.

"My lord, we are introducing this evidence to show her

state of mind—that it was such that she would tell her friend that she was having an affair."

"Relevance, my lord! Mrs. McSweeney's state of mind is not at issue!"

Mistake, thought Nigel. Now you're giving the prosecution a chance to spell it out.

"My lord, the relevance is that if she was telling this friend that she was having an affair, then she may have told others about it, too—and if she told others, they may have talked about it as well, and so on—until word of it may have reached Mr. McSweeney. And that is motive."

"My lord," said Langdon, "If learned counsel for the prosecution has any evidence that the defendant actually knew of this alleged affair, then let them present that—not this idle rumor-mongering."

"Yes, we are getting rather speculative here," said the judge. He thought about it for a moment, then turned to the prosecution. "Mr. Slattery, do you have anything from this witness that would indicate that the defendant actually was aware of the alleged affair?"

"I'm getting to it, my lord."

"Do it now, then."

Slattery approached the witness again. Langdon was so ready to object that he did not even bother to sit down.

"Ms. Stoddard," said the prosecutor. "Did Mrs. McSweeney show you anything to support her contention that she was having an affair?"

"What, you mean like a hickey?" said the witness, and then she laughed.

And so did the press and the public audience. Behind the jury screen, Nigel had forgotten, just for a moment, how much everyone was watching.

"No," said the prosecutor. "I mean, something more . . . lasting."

"Oh, you mean the love letters!"

"She showed you love letters?"

"Yes."

"Letters to her, or letters from her?"

"Letters from her."

"So Mrs. McSweeney told you she was having an affair—and then she showed you love letters that she had written as part of that affair?"

"Yes. She took them right out of her purse and showed me. And then she put them back in."

"Why did she have in her possession letters that she herself had written and had presumably sent to someone else?"

"She said that she had taken the letters back because she was ending the affair."

"Thank you. Nothing further."

The prosecutor went to sit down and the defense barrister moved in so quickly that they almost collided.

"Who was Mrs. McSweeney's counterpart in this correspondence?" said Langdon.

"I'm sorry . . . what?"

"Who was she exchanging letters with?"

"Dearest. I mean, I know that wasn't his name. But that's how she addressed the letters that I saw."

"You saw no actual name?"

"No."

"Did she tell you with whom she was having this alleged affair?"

"No."

"Did she say that she had told Mr. McSweeney of it?"

"No."

"Did she say that she had told anyone else of it?"

"No."

"Did you yourself tell Mr. McSweeney of it?"

"No, of course not."

"So you don't know the who or when or how of this alleged affair, or whether anyone else at all saw the letters that you claim you saw, and yet the prosecution expects us to believe that the defendant knew of it!"

"Objection!"

"I'm sorry, was that a question for me?" said the witness.

"No," said the judge. "Everyone remain calm."

"My lord," said Slattery, "we take exception to the admission of the testimony from this witness. It is all hearsay."

"Exception noted. The witness may step down."

But before she could do so, the bailiff nudged the judge and pointed toward the jury section.

"Oh," said the judge. "Thank you for the reminder, Mr. Walker. Are there any questions from the jury for this witness?"

No one among the main twelve raised hand.

But in the alternates section, Siger was waving his arms like a signal man at a dangerous train crossing. He had a folded paper note in one hand.

"I see we have one question," said the judge, with just a hint of trepidation.

The judge sent Mr. Walker to retrieve the note. The barristers both came forward and conferenced with the judge at his bench.

They all looked at the note, pressed their fingers to their temples, rubbed the wrinkles in their foreheads, stroked their chins—and shook their heads.

The judge looked toward the alternate jury box and said, "Sorry. Interesting observations, but not relevant. Better luck next time."

Siger seemed stunned at the rejection. He sat down quietly.

The judge prepared to file the juror note, and the two lawyers walked back toward their tables. Then Langdon stopped. A revelation. He turned on his heel, went directly back to the judge and asked to see the note again. This time when he read it, he understood—and was so enthused about it that he forgot to ask permission and just immediately approached the witness.

"Ms. Stoddard," he said, reading from the note. "Have you very recently spent several days at a full-body waxing and tanning salon, highlighted your hair for the first time in years, removed your wedding ring, and booked a flight to Ibiza?"

The witness sat back in her chair, astonished, and the prosecutor jumped to his feet.

"Objection! My lord, the witness cannot be subjected to such irrelevant and deeply personal inquiries!"

"I think we did all agree just a moment ago that there was no relevance to this particular set of jury questions," said the judge.

"Yes, my lord," said Langdon. "But I just realized what the note is getting at."

The judge sighed. He cast a very quick, annoyed glance at Siger, and then turned back to the barristers. "These questions don't seem to me relevant to the credibility of the witness. But this is a murder trial, after all. The court will allow the witness to answer."

Everyone now looked toward the witness. And, flustered as she was, the witness answered. "Yes," she said. "I did get waxed and highlighted, and removed my wedding ring, and booked a flight to Ibiza."

"And in your conversation with Mrs. McSweeney about personal relationships, did you mention to her that you were planning to do all those things?"

"Yes, naturally."

"And did you tell her why?"

"Yes, I told her. I'm having a bit of a fling. I'm not embarrassed about it. I am divorced, after all."

"And it was only at that point that Mrs. McSweeney mentioned something regarding a fling . . . an affair of her own?"

"Yes."

"And she told you no specific details about this affair at all, is that correct?"

"That's correct."

"Has it occurred to you that since you had told her of all the things you were doing in connection with the affair you were having, that she might have been just making one up to keep up with you?"

"I'm not sure I understand . . ."

"In some circles, there are some people who are proud of their dalliances, are there not?"

"I suppose some people . . ."

"Are you one of those types of people?"

"No. I don't brag."

"But yet you told Mrs. McSweeney about your affair and everything it involved, did you not? So wouldn't you agree that there is a natural human tendency nowadays to boast about such things and perhaps even pretend to one's best friend that they are real when they are not?"

"Objection!" said Slattery. "This question not only calls for speculation, it suggests a slur on the character of the English people!"

"In what way?" said Langdon. "That an English woman would have an affair? Or that she would make one up to tell her friend about?"

"Both! We are not the French, after all!"

"As you wish. I withdraw the question. But it does seem to me that if the affair is a fantasy, then the notion of my client having a motive is fantasy also. My lord, I'm done with this witness."

The judge turned to the prosecutor.

"Redirect, Mr. Slattery?"

Slattery stood in the center of the courtroom, all eyes on him, and he hesitated. He pushed a lock of gray hair back under his wig. He looked down at the floor—actually to check his fly, but not in such a way that he thought anyone could notice. He sighed. And then he turned half toward the witness and half toward the jury.

He's figured it out, thought Nigel. He knows what to do. It's obvious.

"My lord, we have no further questions," said Slattery. "For not only does the identity of Marlie McSweeney's lover not matter—it also does not matter whether he was even real. Indeed, if he was not, as the defense is suggesting, that merely increases the great tragedy of it all. For if the lover that Mrs. McSweeney spoke of to Carole Stoddard was a mere fantasy—if the letters that Mrs. McSweeney wrote were to someone that she made up from her own imagination, someone to fill the void and the emptiness to which her husband's lifestyle subjected her, someone who would understand her, and sympathize with her, and above all, value her—as she deserved to be valued—and if Liam McSweeney heard the rumors, and believed them, without ever knowing that the lover his wife described in her letters was never anything more or less than the person she had hoped he himself would be—why, that increases the great tragedy of it all—but it does not reduce his motive one whit!"

"My lord, I object!" said Langdon. "No testimony has been introduced to show that Liam McSweeney ever saw the alleged letters, and my learned friend is not asking a question, but merely giving his closing arguments!"

"Indeed he is, Mr. Langdon," said the judge. "Everything after Mr. Slattery's statement of 'no further questions' will be stricken from the record. Members of the jury, you will ignore everything that the prosecuting attorney said after that point. But don't feel that you are missing anything as you erase it from your memory. I'm sure Mr. Slattery is proud of his eloquence and will repeat it all for you when we actually get to the end. The witness may step down."

Mrs. Peabody whispered to Siger.

"My, that was fun. I hope you ask more questions like that!"

10

The next morning at Bob's Newsstand, Nigel saw the headline in *The Daily Sun*: "Alternate Juror Devastates the Prosecution!"

Bob put a lid on Nigel's large coffee and said, "You're going to hurt your neck, the way you twist it in the other direction every time you see a newspaper. I don't want to tell you to get your coffee at the cafe instead, but I'd hate to have to call emergency services."

"I'm that obvious?" said Nigel.

"Yes. Also, Hendricks told me. Also, Lois told me. Also, Rafferty from leasing—"

"I get it," said Nigel. "Everyone knows I'm anonymously on a jury."

"Yes," said Bob. "Say, I didn't know that jurors were even allowed to ask questions the way that fellow did yesterday."

"I can't talk about it," said Nigel.

"Right. No need to apologize. We all know you'll do the right thing."

"Uh-huh."

Nigel took his coffee and got into a Crown Court sedan that pulled to the curb to pick him up.

Twenty minutes later, Nigel walked up the stairs into the corridor for Court 13.

Most of the jurors were already there. A certain natural grouping had begun to take place, as Nigel had expected it would. The twelve primary jurors were mostly gathered closest to the courtroom door, whether standing or seated on the hard benches. But the smaller alternate group had a center of gravity a bit farther down the corridor—although there were a couple of satellite jurors that seemed willing to cross over in conversation from one orbit into another. Lucy was standing a bit apart from both groups—on her mobile phone again.

As Nigel considered which group to attach himself to while waiting, Siger entered from the stairs and came walking quickly toward him. He motioned for Nigel to join him a few steps away at the opposite wall. "May I tell you something confidentially?" he said.

Nigel was surprised at the request, but nodded.

"I saw a newspaper headline before I came in today."

"Yes," said Nigel. "It's difficult not to."

"Do you think the judge will disqualify me?"

"Over the headline? No. Perhaps the newspaper overstepped itself a bit, but you did not. I expect that when it comes time to deliberate, we'll be sequestered, to avoid such issues."

"I didn't intend to cause a problem by asking a question," said Siger. "I don't know at all how I will vote, and I'm not trying to sway anyone in any direction. I only wanted some information. After all, we can't make bricks without clay."

"Interesting you should put it that way. That's a well-known phrase."

"Basic legal principle, is it?"

"No," said Nigel. "What I meant was—well, never mind. Now that I think about it, that is a very sound approach to what we are doing. So long as you keep it in the courtroom."

"Yes. Yes. Of course."

The courtroom door opened, and the jurors filed in. The lawyers and other court officers were already present and ready. The doors closed.

All the jurors took their seats, and after they had done so, Nigel noticed two empty chairs in the primary section.

That could not be good.

Mr. Walker told everyone to rise. The judge entered and immediately turned toward the jury. "You may have noticed two empty spaces among you," he began.

And then he regretfully informed them: earlier that morning, primary jurors numbers eight and nine had become quite ill, and were very sorry, but were, in the words of one of them, "incapable of controlling projectiles of fluids from any of their orifices" and were on their way to hospital. Apparently they had not only partaken of the white cream sauce pasta in the canteen the day before, but had also taken some of it home for a late supper.

A supper they had taken together, the judge added. One more reason to avoid fraternizing.

The court had already sent flowers, and there was no

need for the surviving jurors to send their sympathies—but this meant that two new vacancies had opened among the primary juror group, and so alternates would need to be moved over to complete the twelve.

The judge turned to Ms. Sreenivasan, and she read two numbers from the list.

The first was Lucy. She excused herself from her alternate seat next to Nigel and dutifully took a seat in the primary jury section.

The next number was for the insurance agent in the Lacoste polo shirt. He stood, sighed, and went to occupy the remaining empty primary chair.

"Thank you," said the judge. "Fortunately, we started with five alternates. We still have two. That should more than suffice. But let me make this request of all jurors: don't eat cream sauces that have been left exposed on the counter overnight. Look both ways when you cross the street. Don't run with scissors. We value you, not just for the service you are providing here, but also as individuals—so the court wants you to take care of yourselves, every bit as much as your mum does."

The judge sat back, took a breath, and looked at the lead defense barrister.

"Mr. Langdon, are you ready to call your first witness?"

"The defense is ready, my lord. We call Mr. Percy Pemberton."

Percy Pemberton, in his midfifties, wearing a flannel shirt and khakis, got up from the interior gallery and came forward to the witness box without hesitation, head held high. He spoke clearly and loudly as he was sworn in.

He's on a mission, thought Nigel. Not the impression you want your witness to convey. What it tells the jury is that the witness has an agenda, and therefore he might lie.

The first-chair barrister for the defense, Langdon, Q.C., stood up and prepared to ask his questions. He made a show of staring for a moment at the notes in front of him—as if what he was seeing there was so momentous that he could hardly believe it. He approached the witness.

"Mr. Pemberton, for the last three years, have you been living in a home situated on the east side of Westbury-on-Sea?"

"Yes. I live on the island and work for Mr. McSweeney."

"Where, exactly? Mr. McSweeney owns two properties on the island, does he not?"

"Yes, he has his main holiday estate, and there's also an abandoned Boy Scout camp that he bought a year or so ago, but it's not habitable. They've barely started work on it."

"So you live at the main estate?"

"Yes. I'm the caretaker there. I have my own apartment on the second floor of the main building. I live there year 'round and look after the place, because Mr. McSweeney is generally there only in the warmer months."

"Were you living there in August of last year?"

"Yes."

"Was Mr. McSweeney staying there at that time?"

"Yes. He and Mrs. McSweeney both came out in the middle of the month for a few days holiday."

"On the seventeenth of August, is that right?

"Yes."

"How long did they both stay?"

"She went back on the twentieth. He stayed on for the entire week. I mean, until—until he learned what had happened to her."

"On these holidays, was it typical for Mrs. McSweeney to return to their home in Hampstead before Mr. McSweeney did?"

"Oh yes. Always. They would both come out for a few days to enjoy the weather and red squirrels and such together, and then she would go back and he would always stay on longer to check on his property."

"So Mr. McSweeney was still on the island on the night of the twenty-first before Mrs. McSweeney was killed in the early morning at their home in Hampstead on the following day?"

"Yes. He was at the hotel bar until shortly after nine in the evening, when Mr. Farnsworth from the hotel brought him back to the estate. I saw them pull up in Mr. Farnsworth's car. There are no private vehicles allowed on the island, you see, not even for Mr. McSweeney—so the only transportation is what is provided by the hotel."

"I see. That's true for cars on the island, and it's also true for access by boat, correct? That is, when the tide is high—as it was during that night and early morning—the only way to get to or from the island is by using the one passenger ferry?"

"Yes. Mr. McSweeney is negotiating to be allowed to use his own dock for a boat, but the hotel hasn't allowed it yet. He does have a sea tractor of his own, but you wouldn't want to be on one of those in more than a foot or two of water. The only way that Mr. McSweeney can get to the island at high tide is the passenger ferry from the mainland pub, just like everyone else. And if he tried to cheat and bring a boat of his own across anyway—which he would never do, because Liam McSweeney does not cheat—well, in August it's still high season, and everyone would have seen him do it."

"So you're saying that to get to the mainland that night, he would have had to swim?"

The witness laughed. "Yes, but it's not something I'd want to try."

"So you saw Mr. McSweeney returning to his home at nine p.m. the night before the murder. Did you also have occasion to see him in the morning of August twenty-second—the morning that Mrs. McSweeney was killed at their home in Hampstead?"

"Yes. I saw Mr. McSweeney at seven a.m. Give or take five minutes or so."

"Tell us, please, where it was that you saw him."

"Well, I was taking a walk, you see, along the cliffs, and then I stopped and looked down."

"And?"

"And what, sir?"

"What did you see when you looked down?"

"Well, sir, I saw the water, and I saw the beach, and I saw Mr. McSweeney."

"You saw Mr. McSweeney on the beach below the cliffs, at about seven that morning?"

"Yes."

"What was he doing?"

"He was doing a bit of surfing, sir."

"Surfing? You mean he was surf-riding—as on a board?"

"I mean surfing, sir. Just like the Beach Boys. It's quite the thing on the Devon coast now. The town of Westbury's got a school for it. McSweeney took it up himself this past year."

"So you saw him surfing there, down below the cliffs?"

"Yes."

"Did he see you?"

"Yes, sir. I waved to him, and he waved back."

"He was in the water at the time?"

"Yes, surfing, just as I said—standing on his board, riding the wave, waving back—just like people do."

"Did you go down to the beach to say hello to him?"

"No. It's a bit of a walk."

"Have you ever done that hike yourself?"

"Yes."

"How long does it take?"

"About twenty minutes going down the path; half an hour coming back up."

"So at seven a.m. on August twenty-second, the defendant, Liam McSweeney, was on the beach below the cliffs in a nearly inaccessible part of the island, is that correct?"

"Yes."

"Can you tell us any way that it could conceivably be possible for Mr. McSweeney to be there at that time and also be at his Hampstead residence in London just a few hours earlier when his wife was killed, when we all know that the trip from Hampstead to Westbury-on-Sea by itself takes at least—"

"Objection, my lord," said Slattery, quickly. "Calls for speculation on the part of the witness."

"Sustained."

"I'll rephrase," said Langdon. "We will have later witnesses for that. All we need right now is this: at seven a.m.

on August twenty-second, did you see the defendant on the beach below the cliffs, in the surf, riding a wave on his board?"

"Yes."

"Nothing further."

Slattery stood for the prosecution's cross-examination.

Nigel knew what should be asked; he could barely keep his seat, he was so anxious to hear the question put forward.

"The prosecution has no questions at this time, my lord," said Slattery.

"Very well," said the judge. "The witness may—"

Nigel raised his hand.

"Is there a question from the jury?" said the judge.

All the other jurors looked at each other and shook their heads.

"Yes," said Nigel.

"Write it down and pass it to Mr. Walker, please."

Nigel had already written it, and he passed the note to the bailiff. The bailiff showed the note to the judge. The judge motioned the two barristers to come forward. They looked at the note, and they both looked puzzled. But finally Slattery nodded, and Langdon just shrugged.

"Proceed, Mr. Slattery," said the judge.

The prosecutor approached the witness. "Mr. Pemberton, was the tide in or out when you saw Mr. McSweeney surfing below the cliffs?"

"Well, that's . . . that's sort of relative, isn't it? I mean, it was in enough for there to be water there, that's for certain. Otherwise he'd have been standing in the sand. And you can't ride a board in the sand."

"In which direction was the wave breaking?"

"Ah . . . I'm not sure I understand the question."

"When you saw Mr. McSweeney standing on his board in the water, waving to you, in which direction were he and his board moving?"

The witness sat back and thought about it. He put his hands up in front of him as though visualizing it, and moved them back and forth. Then he pointed to his left. "That way," said the witness.

"To your left, as you were looking down from the cliffs?"

"Yes."

"So he would have been on a wave breaking to the north."

"Ah . . . yes."

"Mr. Pemberton, do you know what the weather reports were for the island on the date in question?"

The witness laughed. "Do I know what the weather report was on that specific date?"

"Yes. Do you?"

"No, sir. I'm not in the habit of committing daily weather reports to memory. Are you?"

"No," said Slattery, looking down at the note that he had received from Nigel. "I myself am not. However, if it were the case that a moist front moved in over the island that night, would it not be likely that dense fog would have formed immediately below the cliffs, making it impossible for you to see anything at all on the beach below?"

The defense barrister leapt to his feet so quickly that he almost got dizzy.

"Objection, my lord! The witness is neither a meteorologist nor an oceanographer, nor is the Crown's barrister, nor is the juror who submitted this question!"

"No," said Slattery, "of course we are not. But these things can be determined."

"My lord," said Langdon, "even the most precise report from the National Weather Service will not tell us exactly what the view was from that precise location on the cliffs at exactly that moment!"

"Enough! I will see all attorneys in my chambers. The jury is excused for a ten-minute recess. Please do not go any farther away than the loo."

Mr. Walker told everyone to rise. The judge and the attorneys snuck away to chambers, and the jury stood and stretched.

As they began to file out, Nigel noticed that more than one of the other jurors glanced up at the wall clock. It was almost noon—and taking a short break now meant they would have to come back and do another full hour, and then be late going to lunch—again.

"I hope we don't end up missing the canteen because of this," said Bankstone.

Nigel ignored that. He watched Lucy walking down the corridor, past the loo, to the exit. Perhaps she was just heading for the vending machines on the next floor.

Nigel did so, too.

But when he turned the corner, she was gone from sight. She should have gone down the stairs, immediately in front of him, which led to the floor with the vending machines.

But Nigel didn't hear any sounds of footsteps on the stairs. He could, however, see that the door at the far end of the corridor was just now closing. He went in that direction. Probably it led to a fire escape.

He would need an excuse to be going out there himself; but that was easy, he'd just say he'd come out for some fresh air.

Unless, of course, she was a smoker and had gone outside to light up.

Well, the hell with it; he'd think of something when he got there.

He pushed the door open and, mercifully, was not immediately hit by the scent of tobacco smoke. That was the good news.

The bad news was that Lucy wasn't there. The person who had snuck out onto the fire escape was Siger. He was standing at the railing, facing the other way, looking downward and across the street. He half-turned at the sound of the door opening. He saw Nigel, and didn't look happy at the interruption.

He took a pipe out of his pocket, with a reddish-brown briar wood bowl . He turned to face Nigel as he prepared to light it.

"Damn chilly air, in my opinion, but when you've got a habit like mine, you take what you get. Anyway, it helps me think. Hope you don't mind."

"Not at all," said Nigel. "I'm not greedy. I just came out for the one breath of air. Time to head back soon anyway."

Siger nodded, and then he put a match to his pipe and turned to face the other direction again. He seemed to be looking down at something in the street, and Nigel stepped up to the railing next to him to have a look as well.

"Something going on down there?" said Nigel.

"What? No, no," Siger said, and Nigel saw no reason to disagree. At least Newgate Street was not full of news vans at the moment. In front of the Viaduct Tavern, a man in a black wool overcoat, having a smoke, turned around and went back into the pub. A clerkish-looking man farther up the street was walking quickly, carrying a document folder. And a man and a woman were walking together in the opposite direction with takeaway lunch bags.

Siger got one puff of smoke out of his pipe, and then said, "I'll be right along."

Nigel went back inside and quickly walked down the corridor. When he reached the stairs, he paused. Maybe Lucy had found an alternate route to the vending machines. If so, she might still be there. He turned and went quickly down the stairs, his footsteps echoing loudly as he went. He reached the bottom of the stairs, just a few steps from the vending machines—and there was no one. No one there at all.

It reminded Nigel of a dream he used to have—that he was in university again, and everyone else was in class, but not him, because he couldn't find the bloody room.

Well, that wasn't a good sign. He hadn't had that dream in a long time, and he had never liked it.

Nigel checked his watch. It was one minute past the hour.

He was late. But not by much. And he was pretty sure there was a shortcut if he took the door at the other end of the corridor.

He ran, not full-on but just a confident jog, to that door, and—locked!

Now it was two minutes past the hour. Nigel turned and

ran full-on back the other way. When he reached the stairs he took them three steps at a time; he emerged on his home floor gasping for air, and hoping to see all the jurors still gathered in the corridor waiting to go in.

But no. The corridor was empty, and the door to the courtroom was closed.

Nigel walked to the closed courtroom, paused to try to get his breath under control—it was too late to do anything about the sweat—and opened the door.

The judge was at his bench. The jury gallery was full of Nigel's peers. The lawyers were all at their tables.

The public gallery was, oddly, completely empty. No family, no spectators, no press.

Which meant something was up.

And all eyes were on Nigel.

"Good of you to join us, alternate juror number five," said the judge.

Nigel walked between the lawyers' tables, entered the jury section—with the little gate creaking loudly—and took his seat.

The judge ignored him now and made a conspicuous pretense of looking at some notes. Lucy, seated at the end of the permanent section nearest Nigel, was finishing off a Mars bar—the type from the vending machine. She leaned forward and whispered to him.

"You should have taken the shortcut, like I did. It's the door at the end of the hall."

"It was locked. Someone must have let it close behind them."

"Oh," she said. "Oops. Sorry."

The judge looked up from his papers and spoke. "Ladies and gentlemen of the jury . . ." He paused. "Good news—the court will again let you all out a bit early. Bad news—I must ask you all to go home and pack your bags."

The courtroom was silent, except for the intake of breath from the jury.

"We don't want to do this, for many reasons, not least of which is the inconvenience to all of you. But issues have been raised in response to a juror's question . . ."

The judge glanced sidelong at Nigel as he said this, but several of the jurors—especially Bankstone—were less subtle and overtly glared.

The judge continued. "Such that we have no choice but to go to the island ourselves and see the view firsthand."

Now there were audible groans.

"We will assemble in the alley at nine in the morning. Do not be late. We want to get there and back again on the same day if we can. We have chartered a bus and we have made arrangements to stay overnight at the island's only hotel if, and only if, it becomes necessary to do so. But we'll try to avoid that. Bring what you think you might need, but only what you can easily carry. Because of the special circumstances, all meals will, of course, be taken care of.

"I daresay the sudden nature of this may be inconvenient for some of you. I remind you that you are English jurors. But if any of you feel you have a reason why you cannot possibly do this, please write it down—briefly—raise your hand, and then pass your note to Mr. Walker."

There was a general rustle, but after a few moments, only two jurors actually raised their hands.

The first was Bankstone.

No great loss, thought Nigel.

The next was Lucy.

Nigel sighed.

Mr. Walker collected the two notes, and took them to the judge, who reviewed them very quickly. The judge called out the number for Bankstone.

Bankstone stood, eagerly.

"Tickets to the London Palladium are not sufficient cause," said the judge. "Even if they are front row seats. Denied. Sit down, please."

Now the judge called out the number for Lucy. She stood. The judge looked at her note, and then at her.

"See if you can work it out," he said. "If you can't, call Ms. Sreenivasan first thing in the morning."

The judge turned back to the entire jury. "Again, nine in the morning, and remember all my cautions. We are adjourned."

All the jurors exited to the corridor in a rush, with confusion and even some grousing.

In the corridor, Siger took his unlit pipe out of his pocket and walked in the direction of the fire escape. Nigel went in the other direction, looking for Lucy. As he reached the stairs to the exit, Bankstone caught up with him. The man was not happy.

"This is what happens when someone asks too many questions," he said. "Now what do I do with these?" He held up his theater tickets.

Nigel shrugged. "Donate them? I'm sure someone in London hasn't seen *Cats*."

Bankstone angrily tore the tickets into tiny pieces, dropped them on the floor like confetti, and stormed off down the corridor.

Nigel continued on and caught up with Lucy just as she was shutting off her phone. He suggested a pint at the Magpie and Stump across the street.

She hesitated, it looked to Nigel like it was yes, and then— it was no. Ballet lessons.

As lithe and limber as Nigel was sure she was, ballet lessons still surprised him.

And, on the theory that the more unlikely the excuse is, the more likely it is intended to convey a rejection, he prepared himself to say good afternoon and be on his way.

But then she said, "Have you noticed that Mr. Siger keeps saying things that Sherlock Holmes said in those stories and films?"

Nigel looked at her in some surprise. Of course he had noticed, but he didn't realize anyone else had. "Yes," said Nigel. "It's rather odd."

"Well, I don't know about odd. But it's a little unusual. At first I thought he was doing it to sort of chat me up. But now I think it's not that—I think he's just such an enthusiast that he wants to share it."

"That's a possibility," said Nigel.

"Is there another?" she said.

Nigel shrugged.

"Well, at least we know he's not a ringer," she said.

"What do you mean?"

"I mean, he's not someone who got onto the jury on purpose, with an agenda. If he were, he wouldn't be calling attention to himself this way."

"True," said Nigel. "But getting a ringer onto a jury is not an easy thing to do in the first place. Not when selection is random and you don't allow all those challenges like they do in America."

"But maybe not so hard if most of the population is favorably disposed to your side to begin with," she said. "And of course you could also convert a juror into your ringer after they are selected, rather than before."

"Yes," said Nigel. "Nobbling is what it's called. Or tampering. And that's why we're supposed to maintain anonymity."

"And how effective do you think that has been?"

"Not very," said Nigel. "But here you are telling me your suspicion—if there is a ringer, how do you know it isn't me?"

She smiled and shrugged.

"How do you know it isn't me?" she said. And then she went on her way.

## 11

Nigel got his coffee especially early the next morning. He wanted to wake up fully before heading for the departure point. He wanted to be alert and capable of clever, potentially seductive, banter with Lucy.

He was too tired to look away from the headlines. And before Bob could even pour, Nigel saw it in *The Daily Sun*. "McSweeney Jury to Take Road Trip!"

Nigel groaned.

Bob poured Nigel's coffee and said, "All packed, are you?"

"I suppose *The Daily Sun* has advice on what I should be taking with me?"

"It says the whole trip was made necessary just because of a trivial question brought up by one of the more annoying jurors on the alternate panel."

"Fine," said Nigel. "That's their opinion."

"The paper also says it has all the details of the site visit, but isn't revealing them because they don't want to piss off the judge."

"Bloody hell," said Nigel. "That better just be bragging. It's one thing if everyone knows we're going on a site visit. It's something else if the media knows where and when and how we're going."

"Maybe there's a leak," said Bob. "Wouldn't be the first time a juror got in bed with the media, would it?"

"No," said Nigel. "It wouldn't."

Nigel stood staring at the headline for a moment. He drank his coffee and woke up a little more. Then he checked his watch. There was probably enough time.

"Bob, I'm going back upstairs and I'm going to toss something out my office window. I need you to watch for it."

"Will it splatter and make a mess on the pavement in front of my newsstand?"

"No, it won't splatter."

"All right then. But if you injure a paying customer, I'll testify for them if they sue."

Nigel went quickly back into Dorset House and took the lift up to Baker Street Law Chambers. Lois was just now settling in at her station.

"There you are," she said cheerily. "Any progress with the young lady?"

"What? Oh, you mean from the jury. Well, so far the answer is no. She's almost always on the phone. I tried twice to set something up, but the first time she had swimming practice and yesterday it was ballet lessons."

"Swimming and ballet?"

"Uh-huh. But Lois, right now what I need is—"

"Nigel, did you check for a ring?"

"Of course. Very first thing. No ring. And no tan line where one might have been removed."

"And I think you told me she applied at first for an exemption from jury service—but didn't get it?"

"Yes. But Lois—"

"Oh my. Oh my. "

"What?"

"Nigel, it's obvious. But if you haven't already figured it out, then you're just fooling yourself, and there's no point in me explaining it to you."

"I don't see . . . Lois, I don't have time to discuss this. I need a piece of paper about the same size and weight as the jury summons that we got last month."

"You mean like the one you threw out the window?"

"Ah . . . yes."

"Oh my. Oh my."

"Would you please stop saying that?"

Lois opened a drawer in her desk and took out a sheet of formal stationery.

"I knew something bad would happen when you did that," she said.

Then she got a red marking pen and quickly drew something at the top of the sheet.

"What's this?"

"That's to make it look like a summons from Her Majesty's Courts Service," said Lois. "And easier to see. In case you're going to do what I think you're going to do."

Nigel nodded and said, "I think we might have a media mole in our jury pool."

"A mole?" said Lois.

"Someone who has been planted by the media to feed them information that should remain confidential. And I have a theory about who. So this is worth a go. At least if the winds haven't changed."

"I'll open the window," said Lois.

She walked ahead of Nigel into his office. She moved the blinds and raised the window.

Nigel folded the sheet of paper into an airplane. Then he sat behind his desk and—trying to do it just as he had the first time—he tossed the invention out the window.

And then he ran quickly to the lift.

"Good luck!" shouted Lois.

Nigel came out of the Dorset House lobby onto Baker Street. He looked in all directions.

Bloody hell, the thing was already gone!

But now Bob called out from his newsstand, "Did you lose another airplane?"

"Yes," said Nigel. "Which way did it go?"

"Where the wind took it," said Bob. "That way."

Nigel ran that way, toward the intersection with Marylebone Road.

And he caught sight of it—just as a cross-draft diverted the document across the street, along with the pedestrians, who had just gotten their walk signal. Nigel saw it get kicked once, accidentally, and that sent it up over the curb, and from there it drifted another twenty yards, until it came to a stop next to the bronze statue in front of Marylebone station.

Nigel ran across the street after it, against the light.

At the foot of the statue, the faux summons got bumped again, and it slid on down into Marylebone station itself, with all the attendant commotion—rushing air, hurried commuters, and vibrations from the trains and the busker musicians who belted out tunes for coins.

It lighted for a moment on the stairs, beneath the peach-colored wall tiles and a new poster for a West End theater revival that was bringing Diana Rigg back to the stage. Nigel ran to catch up with it, but was blocked for a moment by a middle-aged man who had stopped on the stairs in front of the poster, obviously mesmerized, thinking no doubt about that actress in a spy catsuit on the telly forty or more years earlier.

The summons got kicked by someone dodging that obstruction, and Nigel pursued it down another flight of stairs.

He heard the sound of the next arriving train, and the people on the stairs rushing down with renewed vigor; the sheet of paper got kicked again and again, no one paying attention to what it was, until finally the rush of a departing train picked it up a final time, and deposited it into the open saxophone case of a busker who was plying his trade at the stairway juncture between the eastbound and westbound trains.

Nigel stopped in front of the busker, who was belting out "Summertime." Nigel waited for him to finish, and then said, "I haven't heard you here before. Is this your usual station?"

The man shook his head. "A tall, bearded fellow with a

pipe used to play violin here," he said. "But he told me a couple weeks ago that he's found something better to do."

Nigel considered that, chastised himself for not having figured it out earlier, despite the shaved beard, and tossed a two-pound coin in on top of the airplane.

## 12

A full-length premium motor coach waited with engine running in the alley behind the Old Bailey. The diesel exhaust condensed in the cold air and assailed the group of jurors who stood shivering, hands in their coat pockets, in the alley. They coughed in the fumes and flapped their arms to keep warm, and waited anxiously to board.

Uniformed police stood in the street, directing morning traffic away from the alley. The media—in vans, on foot, and on motor scooters—were camped in front of the courthouse but were blocked from entering the alley.

Nigel looked about for Lucy and didn't see her. Her carpool still hadn't arrived.

Now the Old Bailey door opened. The bailiff Mr. Walker stepped out, followed by the witness Percy Pemberton, and then Slattery, Langdon, the judge—and, last, Ms. Sreenivasan the court steward, with a clipboard in hand.

She walked over to the group of jurors and began checking off their names. Then she walked back to the judge and attorneys.

"We're missing three at the moment," said Ms. Sreenivasan to the judge. "But the driver called in and said they are just delayed by traffic; they'll be here within five minutes."

Slattery the prosecutor leaned toward Langdon for the defense and said, possibly in jest, "If they're not here in the next ten minutes, we'll be down to eleven—perhaps you can move for another mistrial."

"Not going to need one. I've already destroyed your motive and provided an alibi. I'm getting an acquittal this time. You're the one who will wish it was a mistrial."

"No one gets a mistrial," said the judge. "We still have jurors to spare. Just as soon as they get here."

"I have dibs on shotgun," said Slattery.

"No such thing," said Langdon. "First in, first choice."

"You're both wrong. My bailiff gets shotgun, and then Ms. Sreenivasan, and then you two sit together behind her."

The judge looked around. Ms. Sreenivasan looked at her mobile phone and nodded, but there was still no car in sight.

"My lord," said Langdon, "in the interests of us all not catching pneumonia, may I suggest that if the remaining jurors do not arrive within the next five minutes, a dismissal would be in order—"

"Oh, please," said Slattery. "My learned friend should just learn to suck it up."

"My lord, I object! My learned friend's tone is—"

"Get ready to board," said the judge. "Here's their car

now. And if you two don't watch your manners and elbows, we'll turn the whole thing around and go right back home."

And indeed, at the far end of the alley, the police barricade had parted, and the constables were waving a sedan on through.

Lucy, Mrs. Peabody, and a third juror got out of the car.

The jurors who had been waiting were told to board. Nigel tried to hang back, waiting for Lucy, but Mr. Walker and Ms. Sreenivasan got behind him and ushered him immediately onto the bus.

Mrs. Peabody settled into the seat next to Nigel. "Would anyone like a wine gum?" she said, holding a package up for all to see.

No one did, at first—but then, as Mrs. Peabody opened the package, Lucy, taking the seat behind her, relented.

"Thank you," said Lucy. As she peeled off a purple wine gum from the roll, she glanced at Mrs. Peabody's purse. "My, you certainly come prepared," said Lucy.

"Yes," said Mrs. Peabody. "I just wish I had remembered to wear my sensible shoes. But I do have a sleeve of Hobnob's chocolate-covered oatmeal biscuits. And my own Earl Grey tea bags, because it has to be Twinings. And my sunscreen, though I doubt I'll need it, given how that sky is shaping up. And my bottle of allergy pills, because who knows what the flora is like on the island. And a pen. And a penlight. I had a penknife, but they confiscated that the first day at the courthouse, so I don't bring that anymore."

"They confiscated my lighter the first day as well," said Siger, seated behind her. "But if I'm allowed an opportunity to smoke, I'm prepared for it."

"Yes," said Mrs. Peabody. "One should always be. As my late husband used to say, for want of a nail, a shoe was lost. And then it went on from there, of course."

The windows were tinted, but the judge wasn't satisfied with that. There were curtains on the windows as well, and he ordered all the jurors to draw them closed before the bus proceeded.

Two officers on motorcycles in front of the bus started their engines, a marked sedan pulled up behind the bus, and then they were ready. The police moved the barricades aside, and the convoy came out of the alley, made a right turn, and then a left onto Newgate Street.

For the first forty minutes, getting out of the city, they might have been just any holiday tour group that happened to have a police escort. But then they reached the M4 and headed west—and within a few moments, a BBC helicopter appeared overhead. And then one for Sky News. And then a couple of motorbikes began suspiciously trailing them from behind.

The bailiff looked out the window and called the judge's attention to their pursuers.

"Yes," said the judge. "And that's why we have curtains."

13

Two miles from the coast of Devon, the bus and its escort took one more turn—and then marked police cars came up behind them and set up the final barricade. This far the media could pursue, and no farther.

The bus continued on, and in a last wheeze of diesel exhaust, came to a stop in the car park in front of the Running Monk pub.

The judge got out first. He wore a pastel cardigan under his open mac, with a white short-brimmed cap, looking very much like a well-off pensioner on holiday. He held one arm out behind him, keeping everyone else in the vehicles, as he surveyed the scene. He looked first at the street in front of the pub—which was clear—and then at the sky directly overhead—which was not.

"What's he doing?" said Lucy, her face up against the glass.

"Extending his middle finger, I think," said Nigel. "At the media helicopters."

Now an officer in one of the marked cars got on the radio, and a few moments later, the news helicopters with their cameras backed off.

The judge and the two barristers stood to one side of the bus, looking nervously about at the road, and the sky, and even the distant sea.

Finally the judge gave the all-clear. The jurors disembarked from the bus and assembled on the pavement in a little huddle with Mr. Walker and Ms. Sreenivasan.

The sign above the pub illustrated its presumed namesake—a plump monk, smiling and jogging in his brown robe and fluorescent Nike trainers.

To the south, the sky was mostly clear over the Devon coast, with only faint white clouds. To the northeast, the clouds were thicker and grayer. The small surf hitting the coast showed the misty blowback of an offshore wind. To the west was one of the several tidal islands for which this part of the coast was famous, and where Liam McSweeney had made his vacation home.

Ms. Sreenivasan pointed in that direction. The island was about a mile away, across the knee-deep water. "That's our destination," she said. "We'll go across shortly."

"Go across in what?" said one of the primary jurors.

"The tide's rather deep, so we're taking the passenger ferry," said Ms. Sreenivasan, with an apologetic smile. "It's at the island right now, but they'll bring it back within the hour. You are all welcome to go into the pub until it is our turn to cross; we don't want you to stand around outside and become a spectacle or catch cold. You may use your lunch allowance here, but you may not use it for alcohol. And if you decide to indulge on your own—no more than a pint each, please. Wait, wait, please, don't everyone rush off yet—one more thing. We have done everything in our power to keep the media away, but we cannot prohibit the locals from enjoying their own pub, so there may be a few inside. You must not fraternize with them. Please remember that you are still a jury, and an anonymous one, and behave accordingly. Thank you."

She smiled and nodded, and all the jurors rushed toward the pub entrance.

Inside the Running Monk pub, the barmaid peeked out the window. "Here they come," she said.

Bert—a local man in his fifties, with a weathered tan, a wool pullover cap, and a slick windbreaker—came over to look as well. "I've never seen a whole courtroom on holiday before," he said.

"Shh," said the barmaid. "Don't spread it around. The poor dears are trying to be a secret."

Bert shrugged and went back to his booth with his beer.

Then the barmaid turned and faced everyone else in the pub—most of whom weren't paying any attention at all. "Everyone," she announced, "when this new group of . . . ah, tourists . . . comes in, please do not talk to them. Especially anything regarding sports or the law. Thank you."

"Can we talk about you then, Maggie?" yelled a local in a middle booth.

"Got any fresh chips made up yet?" shouted another from a back booth.

At the dartboard on the back wall, a man in a golfing

cap tossed a dart and cried out, "Double twenty! That's it! I win again!"

His darkly tanned opponent, wearing the rugby jersey of a New Zealand team, grumbled something, put his own darts away, and brought out a wallet. Several bills changed hands.

"I think this nearly puts my retirement plan back in order," grinned the man in the golfing cap. "G'night, Maggie! My work here is done."

The man in the golfing cap went out the back door, and the man in the rugby jersey came up to the bar to console himself with another pint.

The visitors from the Old Bailey entered the pub. They seated themselves in an instinctive grouping—most of the jurors sat together, the officers of the court keeping to themselves.

On the display wall behind the bar was a black-and-white photo, perhaps a few decades old. Lucy studied it as Maggie brought their lunch specials and a pint each.

"What is that?" said Lucy.

"What, the odd-looking thing in the photo, with the ridiculously big tires, listing to one side with waves crashing into it?" said Maggie.

"Yes."

"That's the sea tractor. Trying to get out to the island during the storm of '96."

"Don't think I've ever seen one of those before," said Nigel.

The barmaid nodded. "That's just another of the lovely things that makes our little tidal island unique. During low tide, you can walk across and not even get your ankles wet. During a very high tide, you can take a shallow-draft boat across, if the weather's decent. But when the tide is at just a certain height—quite a bit lower than it's at right now—you can ride the sea tractor. There are two of them actually, one is for the hotel and our pub, and the other belongs to . . . to Mr. McSweeney."

"Looks like fun," said Lucy. "I can't wait to try it."

"Really?" said Nigel.

"You are with the party that just pulled up in the bus, aren't you?" said Maggie.

"Yes," said Lucy.

"Well then, you won't get to do the sea tractor this time," said Maggie. "It's across at the island right now, and the tide is too deep to bring it over. So you'll be taking the boat instead. Bert will take you across when it's your turn. In the meanwhile, you've arrived just in time for my afternoon tourist welcome speech."

"Must you?" said Bankstone. "We aren't exactly tourists, you know."

Mrs. Peabody looked alarmed at that remark, and she tried to shush Bankstone with an elbow nudge and a whisper. "We're supposed to keep a low profile!"

"Well, I know you aren't locals," whispered Maggie, quite pleasantly, "and I didn't see any paintball weapons and you aren't all giggling like fools, so I knew you aren't on a corporate team-building retreat, either."

"He only meant," said Nigel, "that we are short on time—so perhaps you could give us just the abbreviated version?"

"I'll do my best," she replied, "although I hate to short-change the American tourists. There's at least one here today."

"You mean the man from Las Vegas?" said Siger. "The fellow in the back booth, with his sunglasses on indoors, and wearing alligator shoes that have bits of sand stuck in them, of a type that is more characteristic of deserts than the sea? Sitting across from the dedicated sports enthusiast from New Zealand? Next to a local who, judging from the wear on his face, spends significant time exposed to the elements, and from the wear on his clothes does it as an occupation rather than for recreation, and from his wool pullover cap and his presence in this pub at this hour is quite possibly the water-craft operator who will take us across to the island?"

"Well, yes, as a matter of fact," said Maggie. "That's Bert. And I think you guessed right about the Yank next to him as well; I heard his accent earlier."

Now she reached up and rang a little brass bell that hung over the bar. "Attention, everyone. If you are new to Westbury-on-Sea and want to hear a bit of history and similar things, gather around. If you've heard me before, feel free to put your headphones back on or just tune me out, as you choose. I promise to stop as soon as the season is done.

"First, if you have wondered about the name of our little establishment—well, we used to be called the Pilchard's Scent—because there used to be a packing plant just a mile or so up the coast, and—well, you can imagine, especially those of you with keen olfactories. Fortunately, it was taken down more than fifty years ago, although rumor has it that if you go out to our back lawn and stand in exactly the right place and tilt your head in exactly the proper way, you can get a whiff of it still. Now we call ourselves something else, and I'll get to that in just a moment.

"You've seen that we have a little island across the way, and it has a very nice hotel, almost as famous as the one on Burgh Island, and not very much else by way of modern accommodations. On the one hand, the hotel has indoor plumbing. On the other hand, you can't get mobile phone reception on the island, no matter where you stand or who your carrier is. But the island does have English red squirrels, an endangered species. And it has monastery ruins from the ninth century, when English monks were an endangered species as well. The Vikings raided the island monastery at least three times. Legend has it that the first time, the monks were totally unprepared—so the Norsemen murdered as many as they wanted to for entertainment, then drank all their wine, stole all their bling, looked around for some maidens to ravish but didn't find any, and so departed. On the second raid a decade or so later, the monks were better prepared—they had installed a lookout tower, with a bell that they rang when they saw the longships approaching. So this time when the Vikings stormed in, they had the sport of knocking around a few monks who had armed themselves with wooden cudgels, the fun of breaking holes in walls to find the bling, and when they got down to the cellar to get the wine, they discovered that several of the bare-pated fellows had run down ahead of them, drunk half the casks themselves, and had begun singing songs. Still no maidens this time, either, because the only nunnery within a day's distance was many miles away on the mainland. Even so, the

Norsemen found this trip to be even more fun than the first one, so they spared the monks who had the wisdom to get drunk and sing and only killed the ones who remained upstairs. A bit later in the century they came back to do it again, and this time as they approached, the Norsemen heard the bell ringing from the tower once again, and they eagerly readied their swords for whatever festivities the monks might have prepared for them.

"But when they came ashore—hearing one final clang from the bell as they tromped across the beach—they found no one inside the castle. No monks, no bling, and no wine. Still no nuns or maidens of any kind. And no note on the door, either.

"The visitors from the north were so offended by this discourtesy that they never came back to this island, and took up the hobby of plundering France and Spain instead.

"Now—what do you suppose had happened to all those bare-pated monks? Well, I'll tell you," she said.

"Not that twaddle again, Maggie," said Bert, coming up to put his empty glass on the bar.

"Legend has it that they built a tunnel," she continued.

"Now Maggie, you know that's all just a lot of codswallop."

"Just because no one ever proved it doesn't mean it isn't so, Bert. And you're a fine one to talk. You spent more than a few afternoons scraping around looking for it yourself."

"Not anymore," grumbled Bert. "And I still say it's codswallop." Bert zipped up his full-length slicker and went out the door.

"Don't mind him," said Maggie to the jurors. "He's just out of sorts because he never found anything. And because he has to get the boat fueled and ready with the weather picking up. Anyway, the legend is that the monks built a tunnel, from the island to the mainland, so that when they saw the tall ships coming, they could escape even if the tide was high. And there's also a legend that they built a tunnel to sneak into the nunnery some five miles inland; they wouldn't be the first ones to try that, I'll wager. So I say the legend makes sense. Stay alive, get sex. What stronger incentives would you need to do a little digging?"

"Makes sense to me too," said Nigel.

Siger took out his pipe. Maggie shook her head and pointed to a sign above the bar. "Sorry," she said. "We don't allow it anymore."

"How much time do we have before our transportation is ready?" said Siger.

"Fifteen minutes," said Maggie. "If the weather holds."

"Can I take this out to the lawn in the back?"

"Certainly," said Maggie. "That's what the locals do."

Siger looked at the group of jurors around him. "Shall we stretch our legs a bit?" he said. "I mean, if my pipe won't bother you."

"I gave up cigs the first time I got—I mean—years ago," said Lucy. "But I can put up with a pipe, if it's out in the fresh air."

"I'll join you," said Nigel.

"I'll stay here and have another pint," said Bankstone.

"I'll come along," said Mrs. Peabody.

A few moments later, the outdoors-inclined jurors stood

in the middle of the meadow in back of the Running Monk pub. The meadow was emerald green, punctuated here and there by low outcroppings of yellowish rock and patches of dark earth. It extended some fifty yards to the north, ending at an unimposing wooden fence that marked the edges of the Westbury Resort golf course, which was apparently undergoing some improvements. To the west was the tidal beach, and beyond that was the island.

Siger had his pipe out, but Nigel noticed that he seemed in no particular hurry to actually light it.

"Ah, this is better," said Siger. "Now my joints feel alive again. I'll just step over there to fire this up."

"You don't need to do that," said Mrs. Peabody, but the man moved a few yards away despite her dispensation.

"You can certainly smell the ocean here, can't you?" said Lucy. "Much more than out front in the car park."

"Yes," said Mrs. Peabody. "Although it's not what I would call a pleasant scent. More like rotting seaweed."

"Yes," said Nigel. "Although I don't see any seaweed."

Siger had his pipe in full flourish now. He exhaled a couple of respectable smoke rings. He watched them dissipate in the breeze, and then he walked back to the others and put out his pipe. "I hope I was far enough away to not disturb you," he said.

"Not a problem," said Nigel. "But I could have told you which way the breeze is blowing from the way the waves are peeling back."

If Siger knew what Nigel was getting at, he didn't show it. He just sniffed the air, and grimaced slightly.

"See? Mr. Siger doesn't like it, either," said Mrs. Peabody.

Siger turned his pipe upside down, tapped it to empty the contents, and kicked the dirt lightly where the ashes fell. "I think it's time for us to get back," he said. "We don't want to miss our boat ride."

As they entered the back door of the pub, they were approached by the New Zealander in a rugby shirt, who was now well into his cups. He went up to Lucy as soon as she came in the door.

"Did you go out for a smoke, miss? Should have told me; I'd have gone with you."

"No fraternizing," said Nigel, pushing in between.

"No what, mate?"

"You're intruding," said Nigel. "Go away."

The man glared but stepped back, just a little unsteadily.

At the front of the pub, the steward and the bailiff had entered.

"Time, everyone, please!" said Ms. Sreenivasan. "I mean everyone who is on the jur—I mean everyone who came in on the bus! Our boat is ready!"

Mr. Walker began to stride through the pub to make sure all the jurors were accounted for. He paused for just a moment at a table where several jurors were finishing their beers.

The bailiff frowned when he saw that empty glasses had accumulated, especially near the insurance agent in the Lacoste shirt, who was just now waving to the barmaid for another.

"You've had enough, lad," said the bailiff.

"You're not my mum," said the man, who wouldn't have said this to the imposing bailiff if he had not already had one too many. "If you want to leave me here, it suits me."

The bailiff reached down, pushed the remaining glass of beer away, and said, "If you are too inebriated to continue, and I tell the judge, he will not only remove you from the jury, he will find you in contempt and throw you in jail. Think about it."

The insurance agent looked up, saw the serious look on the bailiff's face, and nodded. "All right then," he said. "If you say I've had enough, Mr. Walker, I've had enough."

Bankstone and Armstrong were huddled together in a booth, on their second or third pints. Bankstone was shaking his head. "No. You must stay away from public offerings. And I'll tell you why: there are people like me getting in early, and then there are even more people like me trading milliseconds ahead of you every day for every individual stock on the market. You can't beat us. The only thing you can do is this: index funds."

Armstrong considered it, nodded, and raised his glass. "To index funds, then!"

"Damn right!" said Bankstone. "Index funds!"

Mrs. Peabody smiled as she passed by them. "I'm so glad they're getting on," she said.

Ms. Sreenivasan held the door open for the jurors to exit the pub, and a blast of cold air greeted them. "Everyone zip up!" she shouted. "It's getting nippy!"

Outside on the beach, just a few yards beyond the car park, the ferry—a twenty-five-foot, shallow-draft water taxi with a blue canopy over a narrow seating area—was now tied up at the little dock.

Ms. Sreenivasan and Mr. Walker herded the jurors in that direction. The judge and barristers were already there, looking at the boat and talking with Bert, whose attitude clearly said that whoever they all might have been back in London, they were in his world now.

"We're going in that?" whispered Mrs. Peabody.

"She's more than seaworthy," shouted Bert. "I patched her myself just last week."

Mr. Walker and Ms. Sreenivasan stood at the edge of the dock and helped the jurors onto the boat. The group boarded quickly at first, and then began to take longer as they crowded in and the seating logistics became complicated.

Finally all the jurors were in place, and then the judge, the lawyers, and Percy Pemberton stepped on board.

"All right then, off we go," said Bert. He untied the mooring rope and started to go toward the helm.

"Wait," said the judge. "My bailiff and steward are coming, too."

"Afraid not, guv," said Bert. "We're already at capacity once you stepped on. We can't take another soul."

"Then you'll come back and get them and bring them across, too, as soon as you drop us off?"

Bert looked at the sky, and then at the choppy waves, and shook his head. "Not likely. The wind is picking up. I'll be lucky to get back to the dock myself before we have to tie her up for the night."

"I can't manage all these jurors by myself!" said the judge in an impassioned plea. "It's like herding cats!"

Bert looked at the group of jurors trying to arrange themselves in the little boat, and he nodded—what the judge said was painfully obvious. "All right then," said Bert. "I'll take a chance, and make an exception. You can bring one more. Her." Bert was pointing at Ms. Sreenivasan. "That other fellow is way too big."

The judge looked at his steward and bailiff, who both nodded agreeably. Ms. Sreenivasan stepped onto the boat—and Mr. Walker stepped back onto the dock.

"Off we go then," said Bert.

**14**

At the top of the island hotel, the turret widow's walk had a fresh coat of white paint, and so the manager, Mr. Farnsworth, had to be careful. It wasn't a true widow's walk—it looked out the wrong way for that, east toward the mainland rather than out to sea. It was a "tourist turret," Mr. Farnsworth liked to say, and he meant it in two ways – for tourists to visit (during the proper hours, from ten to two only) and pretend to be spies or illicit lovers, and for him to visit at all other hours, and spy just for the fun of it on the incoming and outgoing tourists.

He made sure that the sleeves of his jacket were gathered in close. It wouldn't do to brush up against the railing.

From this vantage point, he could see the passenger boat when it departed from the mainland, and yes, there it was—just now embarking.

He wondered if this group had bothered to check the weather report. Even if they hadn't, if they knew the island like Farnsworth did, they would have looked up and noticed the heavy gray mass drifting in, and the hotel's colored pennants fluttering. Whitecaps were already beginning to form all around the island.

And if they had checked the almanac, they would be aware that the storm coming in was riding with an unusually high tide—which meant that instead of being at least partly accessible to foot traffic at low tide, the island would, for the next twenty-four hours, be entirely surrounded by water, and rather rambunctious water at that.

These weather conditions would have deterred any ordinary group. But he knew this group was not ordinary. He adjusted the focus on the telescope and saw that most of the passengers on the boat were sensibly sitting under the canopy, but two individuals were visible on the outside.

One of them, a tall man, stood at the bow, with his shoulders hunched against the wind, calmly smoking a pipe. The other was leaning over the side rail in the way that people do when they don't quite have their sea legs—or stomach, either.

Farnsworth smiled at that—always a great entertainment, at least from a proper distance. He had seen enough to know that it was the expected group. He turned and went back down the stairs.

15

Nigel wiped his mouth and tried to gather himself up from the railing. He tried to ease his vertigo by looking toward the shoreline of the little island. Even this close, no more than a mile to go, he could see both ends of it. He tried to find one specific distant object to focus on. To his right, at the top of the hotel, he saw something that glinted—and then it was gone.

That was no good. He felt even dizzier than before. He still didn't understand why standing on a boat would do this to a person, but riding a surfboard—a skill he'd learned when he was in Los Angeles and it was just a short drive up Pacific Coast Highway to Malibu—would have the opposite effect.

Paddling out on a longboard was invigorating, not dizzying. Floating at the edge of the surf line was calming. And catching a wave was more of a thrill than almost anything else he knew.

At least it had been, when he was still in Los Angeles with Mara.

But then Mara had gotten an offer for an exhibit in New York, and had decided it was time for a permanent move. The morning after Nigel learned that it was not her plan that he go with her, he'd gone up to Malibu to shake it off. The surf would do that for you, focus your mind, put your body back in touch with the physical world, and break you out of whatever funk you might be in.

But then he'd made a mistake in the water. He didn't really have his focus back, not quite. On a day when the sets were just barely head high, he'd gotten careless, turned his back—and when he saw the rogue wave, rising behind him, it was just an instant too late.

He'd gone under, and stayed under, with the turbulence churning above him, longer than he'd ever been. When he had finally come up, his leash was broken, his board was gone, and it turned out to be a bloody long swim getting back in.

He'd gone back home that afternoon to a house where Mara had packed and gone to New York—and the next day he booked his own flight back to London.

16

The boat was getting very near the island now, with Nigel still at the rail. Bert shouted to him from the helm, with a sadistic grin.

"Don't care much for boats, then?" he said.

"Never have," said Nigel. "Is it always like this?"

Bert nodded sagely. "At least once every twenty years or so. I can't say much for the timing of your tour group. This is the highest tide in years, and anyone can see there's a storm coming in. Normally you can just take the little sea tractor across. Not today."

Now the engine stopped, with a final belch of carbon monoxide to make Nigel even dizzier, and the boat bumped up to the dock.

Nigel didn't wait for it to get tethered. He jumped immediately onto the relatively solid comfort of the wooden dock. The wind was picking up, with intermittent drops of a chilly rain. Nigel adjusted the collar on his mac and looked about.

With the high tide, there was virtually no beach at all. The mooring was at the rocky base of a hundred-foot cliff. The short dock connected to a narrow paved road, which split off in two directions. One branch wound in an S-curve up to the 1930s-style stucco hotel, and the other branch, even narrower, climbed up the cliffs in the opposite direction.

Three vehicles—a passenger van and two sedans—were driving down that road now from the hotel to the dock.

Ms. Sreenivasan, always smiling and not the least bit bilious, helped the jurors get from the boat onto the dock. "Lovely day, everyone, if you brought your umbrellas," she proclaimed. "Mind your step."

The judge came out, followed by the lawyers and the witness Pemberton.

The vehicles from the hotel pulled up to the dock—the passenger van first, and the two cars directly behind it. A portly man, wearing an apricot ascot and a sky-blue blazer with slight grazes of white paint on the elbows, got out of the driver's side of one of the sedans, walked directly up to the judge, and spoke with an accent that was upper class and professionally cheery.

"I'm Farnsworth. Welcome to our humble little island. I hope that you are Mr. Justice Allen?"

"I am. And I have brought the rather large group we spoke of."

"Of course. We have both your vehicles ready. And you're in luck—it isn't quite high season yet. If it does turn out that you must stay the night, you and each of the barristers will have your own rooms. The jurors would have to share, of course."

The judge nodded. "If it comes to that."

"You know," said Mr. Farnsworth pleasantly, "I read a story once about a man who had a dinner party at a place such as this and all of his guests got murdered."

"Thank you for the idea, but these aren't dinner guests, they are my jurors," said the judge. "And I don't intend to murder them. Unless they get especially unruly."

"Do you want to bring everyone back to the hotel to freshen up a bit?"

The wind was picking up, and the judge looked up at the moving clouds. "No," he said. "I want to go directly to the site and get this done as quickly as possible, while the weather holds."

"Very well, we do have something blowing in, no question about it. Constable Bailey came across earlier, and he will drive the van for you."

"I had to leave my bailiff behind, so if you have any additional personnel to help keep my jurors in line, I would appreciate it."

"No, there's no one else—just the one constable."

"Herding skills are all that is needed. A former nursery school teacher? A shepherd?"

"I'm afraid I don't have anyone else at all to send. Aren't your barristers up to it?"

The judge nodded in the direction of the two barristers, who were both busy on the dock, primping and checking the condition of their clothes.

"Oh. I see," said Farnsworth. "Well, I am sorry, but there just isn't anyone else at the hotel besides the cook and one maid. You'll have to make do. Come this way. As you know, we don't allow private cars on the island. I brought you the two vehicles from the hotel. This is all there is. You'll be snug as sardines, but it's a short trip."

They all moved toward the van and the available sedan.

Constable Bailey—a well-fed man in his forties—got out of the van and opened the side doors. "It seats fourteen passengers, in a pinch," he said. "How do you want to do it?"

The judge and Ms. Sreenivasan looked at the minivan—which, if not luxurious, appeared to be at least capable of getting up the hill. The sedan looked as though it had been brought out of a shed and dusted off a bit just for this occasion.

"Most of us will fit in the van," said the judge. "But the last six jurors will have to go in the sedan."

Everyone else took their places in the van. The six remaining jurors all held back, eyeing the sedan suspiciously. It was an older Italian model, with bench seats in both front and back, theoretically capable of seating six. But that was advertising theory, and probably a bit optimistic.

Ms. Sreenivasan dangled the car keys in front of them. "One of you can drive a manual transmission, I hope?" she said.

No one responded immediately. Nigel had never driven a manual. He'd been a Londoner all his life, except for his two years off and on in Los Angeles, and he had never found that skill to be a requirement.

They all looked at each other for a moment—and then finally Lucy nodded.

"We're all set then," said Ms. Sreenivasan, handing her the keys. "Just follow our van!"

Lucy got in the driver's side. Nigel moved quickly to get in next to her.

But not quickly enough. Siger was there first, holding the passenger door open for Mrs. Peabody, and then he got in after her.

"I think I'd better take the front," he said. "Or my knees will be pushing through the top."

Nigel wanted to point out that his own knees wouldn't be all that comfortable, either, but it had started to rain in earnest, and in any case it would seem petty in front of Lucy. He squeezed into the back with Armstrong and Bankstone, all of them holding in their knees and elbows as if seated in the midsection of coach on a transatlantic flight.

Lucy started the car. There was an initial crunch of gears as she tried to put it into first and got third instead—and then another crunch as she tried in another location—but on the next try she got it in gear, and with just a little spinning of wheels in the mud that was beginning to form, they whirred up the initial slope in pursuit of the van.

As planned, they reached the top of the slope with the van still in sight. Then it took a right turn—heading along the east side cliffs, toward some destination not yet in view.

"I do hope they know where we're going," said Mrs. Peabody.

The gears crunched again as Lucy tried to downshift to go up the next rise. The sedan struggled, but maintained momentum.

"You'd think the hotel would have four-wheel drive available, for roads like this," said Bankstone.

"You'd think," said Armstrong.

They continued, with the rain and mud increasing all the while, up the narrow road that traced the perimeter of the cliffs.

"There it is," said Siger.

"There what is?" said Nigel.

"See the stack of rocks above that promontory ahead of us?"

"Yes."

"That's the remains of the wall from the old monastery that our pub hostess talked about."

"You're an archeologist, then, in real life?" said Nigel.

"Well, no—but I did my homework."

"Homework?" said Nigel.

"Of course. I saw it on the Internet when I looked up McSweeney's estate."

"Oh my," said Mrs. Peabody.

"Oh my—what?" said Siger.

Mrs. Peabody shrugged. "Well, it's not for me to say, certainly."

"What isn't?" he said.

"She means that as a juror, you're not supposed to do outside research," said Nigel. "Especially on the bloody Internet."

"Oh," said Siger. He thought it over for a moment, then said, "Oh, you thought I meant that I looked it up after I got on the jury? No, no—I didn't do that at all. I looked it up well before."

"For any particular reason?" said Nigel.

"Um . . . no. I just . . . like to look things up."

That sounded odd, but Nigel let it go.

"Eventually the ruins and the land around it were acquired by a nature conservancy," said Siger, as though digging a deeper hole would help. "They leased their part of the island to a Scouting organization, who built a lodge back in the fifties, not far from the ruins. McSweeney came along a couple of years ago and built his own holiday estate on the island, but he wanted more—and when he saw the abandoned Scout camp, he offered so many bloody millions for it that the conservancy sold it to him. So he's allowed to build on the Scout camp when he wants to, but he is required by contract to leave the ruins alone."

"Well," said Mrs. Peabody, "at least none of that has anything to do with the case. I suppose we won't have to turn you in to the judge."

"Oh!" said Lucy.

She suddenly swerved the car hard to the left. Mud flew from the wheels as she braked, and the car rocked steeply, mashing the passengers together to one side.

They came to a stop. It was a hairpin turn, and Lucy had barely seen it in time.

Nigel looked out his window and saw that they were within a foot of the cliff precipice. Immediately below was a hundred-foot drop, onto hard black boulders and crashing waves. Just beyond the curve ahead of them was a deep gorge, and a narrow wooden bridge that traversed it. The red taillights of the van were crossing that bridge now.

Lucy tried to put the sedan back into first gear; the gears crunched, and the wheels spun in the mud. "Sorry," she said, as she tried again. "My fault. I took my eyes off the road for just a moment. I was trying to look at the ruins we're all talking about."

"Not to worry," said Nigel, peering over the edge. "When we get back to earth, I'll tell you all about the view you missed."

The car got just enough traction to move forward, and the jurors gave a unanimous sigh of relief. They held their breaths again as they drove across the very splintery, minimalist bridge. Then they continued on for another quarter mile.

Finally they reached a relatively broad and level outcropping—where they saw the van, already parked.

"We did it!" said Lucy. "Flat land!"

Rain was pouring down. As they got out of the Fiat, Nigel moved toward Lucy's side of the car to include her under his full-sized golf umbrella—but she apparently didn't notice; she opened a collapsible one from her purse and walked past him.

Nigel, caught flat-footed, pretended for a moment that he had only come over to get a better view of the ruins on the summit behind them. Siger appeared to be doing that too.

Now the constable was shouting at them to join the rest of the group.

Everyone was huddled together near the beginning of a promontory that jutted some fifty yards out into the sea.

"This is the place!" Pemberton announced loudly. He seemed proud of himself.

The wind, the rain, and the sound of surf crashing below the cliff made it difficult for anyone to be heard.

Slattery, the prosecutor, shouted at the witness, "Surely you're not suggesting that you stood here and saw the defendant? The beach isn't even visible from here!"

"Objection!" yelled Langdon. "Argumentative!"

The judge shook his head angrily and shouted at both barristers. They cupped their hands to their ears, turned toward the judge, and yelled, almost in unison, "What?"

"I said, enough!" screamed the judge, as loudly as he could. "We are not taking either testimony or cross-examination at this moment! We are simply trying to suss out where we need to stand in order to see what we need to see!"

"Out there!" shouted Pemberton. "You need to stand out there. That's where I was. On those black rocks!"

He was pointing at the far end of the promontory, which narrowed to a cluster of slick boulders, no more than ten feet across.

"Of course," screamed Pemberton helpfully, as the wind blew sheets of rain at the little group, "the weather was a bit more pleasant at the time!"

This might not be a good idea, thought Nigel. And he was beginning to not like Pemberton.

The judge seemed to have his doubts as well. He shook his head, and shouted something at Ms. Sreenivasan. She nodded. She and Constable Bailey proceeded to hustle all of the jurors back to the van, where they tried to all push inside and huddle out of the rain.

The judge and the two barristers walked out toward the rocky point. They stopped within a few feet of the edge of the promontory. They conferred. The witness shouted and pointed even farther out, to the absolute narrow end of the promontory. The judge looked in that direction, his coat collar turned up, and the wind violently blowing his wisps of white hair. He shook his head.

There was more shouting and gesturing from both barristers—and from the witness, still standing nearer the safer part of the promontory—and then, finally, the judge nodded.

The judge and the barristers returned now to the van, and the judge stuck his head in, with the two lawyers trying to look over his shoulders. "We have two choices," he shouted, and then he brought his voice down a bit, realizing that inside the vehicle he could be heard. "We can return to the hotel, spend the night on the island, and hope that the weather clears tomorrow. Or we can put up with the wind and rain, go out and see the lovely view now, and with any luck, head back to the mainland tonight. What is your preference?"

"Let's get it over with!" shouted Bankstone.

"Show of hands?" said the judge.

It was almost unanimous. Everyone raised their hands except Nigel—partly because he wasn't quite certain that slick rocks on a rainy and windy day was a good idea—and partly because the prospect of spending the night in a resort hotel in close proximity to Lucy seemed like not a bad thing.

"Thirteen to one, that's a consensus," said the judge. "Now, here are your instructions. You will come out onto the promontory as far as can be done safely, to get a view from the position where the witness claims to have been. We will do this in small groups, and for safety's sake, you will go no farther toward the edge than where Constable Bailey and I will be standing. You will have three seconds to look, no more, and then, I want you to go directly back to our vehicles and get out of the rain. Any questions?"

No one truly wanted to get out of the warm dry van. The wind was nearly thirty knots now, and the rain was pelting down in near horizontal sheets. But no one raised their hand.

"Let's get started then," said the judge.

"Slickers at the ready, if you've got them," shouted Ms. Sreenivasan, with completely unwarranted cheerfulness, because few had brought slickers. Only the two sturdiest umbrellas of the group were of any use; the compact collapsible ones did exactly what they were designed to do— expand, and then immediately collapse.

Constable Bailey was wearing an actual full-length mac, and he gallantly removed it, handed one end of it to Ms. Sreenivasan, and the jurors huddled together in a sort of phalanx—with the constable's expanded mac at the front and the two surviving umbrellas—including Nigel's—on either side. The jurors did their best to take shelter behind them as they marched out.

They slogged on orange-brown mud, past low-lying scrub plants, toward the outcroppings of slick, black, lichen-colonized rock at the far end of the promontory.

They proceeded some twenty yards in that direction— and then the judge raised his hand, and the entire group paused. "We can do it in small groups," he said to the constable. "It's too narrow for the whole group all at once. So just a few at a time. Walk out to where the witness is standing now, look down over the edge, and then, just walk on back."

"Are you sure it's safe to do this?" shouted Nigel.

"Of course it is!" Pemberton yelled as loudly as he could. "Just mind your step, and Bob's your uncle!"

Nigel was doubtful. He was pretty sure he had no uncle. And he knew that rocks on the water's edge get adopted by invisible slime and you don't know it's there until you are slip, sliding away.

And he wasn't the only one hesitating.

"You first," said Lucy, standing behind him.

Nigel wasn't sure whether she was addressing him or the constable, but he didn't want to seem unduly timid, and he began to take a step forward.

"No, no, no," said the defense attorney. "Primary jurors first. Then the alternates."

"Why do you suppose the primary jurors have to go first?" said Lucy.

"Because the weather is getting progressively worse," said Nigel. "And the primary jurors are more valuable."

And it was indeed getting worse. Constable Bailey walked the first group of four jurors out onto the promontory—with wind howling, rain slashing, and waves crashing below—and they all came gladly back two minutes later. When the second group walked out, the wind had already increased by several knots, and they hurried back in less than a minute, chased by sheets of rain.

"Next!" shouted Constable Bailey. He could hardly be heard at all over the wind, but his lips were moving and his gestures made his intent clear—he wanted Nigel and the remaining jurors to take their turn now, and walk out onto the promontory.

Nigel shouted back at the constable, "This isn't safe!"

Nigel realized that no one more than four feet away could hear him; he shook his head emphatically, gestured out toward the sea, and made a motion like a wave crashing.

The judge, who had now returned to the area of the vehicles, saw this, looked out toward the rocks, and hesitated. But the constable looked back at Nigel, shook his head, and made a gesture to suggest nice, calm little waves no more than knee high.

And to suggest Nigel was a wimp.

The barristers, standing at a safe distance, glared at Nigel, and gestured emphatically toward the far end of the promontory.

"Quickly now!" The constable shouted at Nigel and the remaining jurors. "While the seas are calm!"

Nigel thought that ship had already sailed. But the insurance agent—who during all this had been paying more attention to a flask he had concealed in his coat pocket—looked up.

"Bloody hell," he said, looking around at the others. "Let's just get it over with."

And with that he strode boldly, if a bit unsteadily, out onto the promontory.

The constable took advantage of that initiative and immediately summoned Lucy, Bankstone, and Siger as well, with Nigel and Mrs. Peabody right on their heels.

Nigel walked deliberately just to the right side of Mrs. Peabody, positioning himself between her and the slick, sloping boulders of the cliff. She seemed a bit wobbly on the heels she had worn. Nigel hoped it wouldn't be necessary to catch her, but he felt obliged to be ready.

Constable Bailey stood boldly in the wind and rain, gesturing to them all to hurry forward. The witness, still at a safer distance, pointed to where the jurors were to position themselves—at the very edge of the rocks.

"You first!" shouted Nigel, and this time, all the other jurors followed Nigel's example, and halted—until the witness himself stepped cautiously onto the rocks, using Constable Bailey as a shield, and pointed below.

"There," he said, pointing down at the surf. "I was standing right here, and down there is where I saw McSweeney!"

The witness then hastily stepped back.

The insurance salesman stepped up to look, followed by Lucy. He glanced down, barely, then took two quick steps back. Lucy took a moment longer at the edge—actually looking to see, rather than just pretending to—and Siger stepped up next to her and looked down as well. Then they, too, stepped back.

Mrs. Peabody and Nigel both approached the edge.

"No," said Nigel, as Mrs. Peabody started to go to the very edge of the rock to look down. "You're already close enough. I know it might look safe, but trust me—it's a slip-and-slide. The rock is covered in slime; you just can't see it."

"Oh," she said. And just as she said it, her front foot did indeed begin to slide. But Nigel already had her by the elbow.

"Thank you," she said.

She stepped back, and now Nigel looked out over the

edge himself. He saw what he'd expected to see—a cauldron of crashing waves directly below them. But he looked farther out. Some twenty yards farther up the beach was a natural rock reef—causing the surf at that specific location, and only at that location, to well up into a shoulder, which broke gradually—and very powerfully in the current conditions—toward the south.

No one was attempting to ride it today, in the windy conditions. On a good day, for an experienced surfer, it could be rideable. Not wise or likely for someone of McSweeney's limited experience, but theoretically rideable.

But to the south only, in Nigel's opinion. That was the only direction in which the break could go, given the shape of the reef. Not toward the north as the witness had said McSweeney was riding. But to the south.

Which meant that the witness could not have seen what he said he saw. It was impossible.

Nigel turned his head to look back at Pemberton, to see if the man had realized that his false testimony had now been revealed—at least to Nigel.

But then came the rogue wave.

Nigel had known it was possible, even likely at some point—but he hadn't seen it coming. Even though he had been looking out at the surf line just seconds before, he hadn't seen it. It was the very nature of such waves in a storm. If you fled from the surf every time you thought you saw one possibly forming, you would never so much as put foot in the water, or sit on the beach, or stand on a rocky cliff. But if you turned your back or looked away—well, then heaven help you.

It was head-high when it hit the rocky tip of the promontory. If it had been any higher, the main force of the wave would have been enough to wash every one of them into the sea.

For an instant, the spray by itself blanked everything out—no one could see anything but the salty water striking their eyes.

And on the slick black rock, Nigel's feet went out from under him.

He hit face-first on the slimy boulder on which he'd been standing. He instinctively reached for the narrow crevice where that boulder lined up with another. He found it—with just his fingertips—barely enough, for the moment.

The water rushed back now from the promontory rocks to the sea. It pulled at Nigel's legs, and Nigel held on—but he sensed something—or someone—to his right side being dragged away.

Nigel reached out with his right hand—while his left still clung desperately to the crevice—and he tried to grab whoever was sliding past him. He caught hold of an edge of peach-colored cotton cloth. But only an edge. In an instant it was torn from his grasp.

The water subsided. Nigel pulled himself up onto his hands and knees. All around him he heard groans, and some curses.

And then a woman's scream.

Nigel struggled to his feet. He shook the salty water from his face and looked.

Where before there had been five individuals standing on the rocky promontory with Nigel, now there were only four. The constable, who somehow seemed to have kept his feet through all of it. Mrs. Peabody and Siger, who had both fallen, but far enough in from the slick rock to not slip away. And Lucy—still on her hands and knees, but near the edge of the rock—and looking down. It was she who had screamed.

Nigel joined her there and looked down as well.

Some fifty feet below, the body of the insurance salesman lay on a shoreline boulder. The collar of his peach-colored Lacoste shirt was turning red. The incoming and outgoing waves moved his arms like a broken puppet and washed blood from his head into the white froth.

He was faceup, and Nigel could see that there was no doubt. There would be no rescue, no resuscitation; the only possibility was recovery—and that possibility was limited.

Constable Bailey came over now and looked down. "Everyone stay back!" he shouted.

The judge came running out to the vantage point now, and probably would have slipped himself, but the constable and Nigel stepped in and slowed him down. They all looked over the edge, along with Lucy, who hadn't budged.

"If we wait for help," said Nigel, "another wave is going wash him away."

"We have a rope and blanket in the van," said the constable, looking down at the body. "We can make a sling. I will go down and get him, if someone will pull him up from above."

It was a brave offer. The face of the cliff was a straight vertical drop—challenging for professionals, but impossible for the untrained.

"I'll go with you," said Nigel.

"I won't risk more juror lives over the one we've already lost," said the judge. "Get what we need from the van. Only Constable Bailey goes down. You can help the officers of the court—our two barristers and myself—pull him up."

## 17

The remaining jurors huddled in their vehicles for shelter from the rain, with Ms. Sreenivasan making sure they didn't budge.

Nigel, and Langdon, who didn't have much bulk but was fit, pulled on the rope, with the judge and Slattery backing them up.

Slowly, painstakingly, with Constable Bailey clinging to the slick rocks and guiding the sling—and with the rope tied to him as well—they pulled the body of the insurance salesman to the top of the cliff. Nigel and the constable carried it back to the van. Jurors in the back moved forward and scrunched together to make room.

The judge was on his mobile, almost screaming into it to be heard over the wind and rain.

Nigel returned to the sedan. This time he was in the front, beween Lucy and Mrs. Peabody. Siger, Bankstone, and Armstrong were in the back.

"Are they calling for a helicopter?" said Mrs. Peabody.

"Yes, but they're not getting one, not in this weather," said Nigel. "Even the news helicopters have gone home, and that was an hour ago, in less wind. And the hotel doesn't have a boat large enough to go out in this wind and surf. So they'll have to take him back to the hotel in the van, no other choice."

"The judge looks very distressed," said Lucy, sitting in the driver's seat of their sedan.

"I think he feels responsible," said Nigel. "And regardless of what he feels, the Crown will probably find him so. Never mind that the fellow was half-drunk."

"Odd how things happen in the force of nature, isn't it?" said Siger. "The insurance man had completed his viewing, and was standing farther from the edge, toward the center of the solid land. You and Mrs. Peabody were much closer to the edge. Yet it was the insurance man who fell to his doom."

"Oh my, you're right," said Mrs. Peabody. "There's just no telling, is there?"

Now the constable came running over to their car, through fierce wind and rain, and he rapped on Nigel's window. Nigel lowered it; a sheet of water blew in.

The constable shouted and waved his arms toward the road on which they'd driven in. "We're going back. Right now! Turn around! We're all heading back. Back to the hotel!"

Nigel rolled the window up and Lucy started the car. The constable dashed back to the van, which was already chugging exhaust fumes and beginning its turn.

The van got out onto the road first. The sedan tried to

follow. Its wheels spun in the deepening mud, Lucy struggled with the gear shift, and finally they got out onto the
road.

It was dusk now. The van was nearly a quarter mile ahead,
its tail lights barely visible through the sheets of rain.

"Shouldn't we be right with them?" said Mrs. Peabody.

"I am trying," said Lucy, and Nigel knew that she was.
There was only so much that the four-cylinder front-wheel-
drive sedan could do.

They rounded a curve. On one side was the beach cliff; on
the other was a steep rise that led to higher ground; and
in front of them, the road was descending toward a narrow
canyon that they had crossed when they first drove out from
the hotel's boat dock.

"We must be getting near the bridge," said Nigel.

"I don't see it," said Lucy.

"Neither do I," said Nigel, staring with her into the fog
and rain. "But I think I see taillights . . ."

It was just a glimpse of the vehicle ahead of them, which
had just crossed the bridge and was starting up the other
side. But now Nigel stopped talking. He'd heard an ominous
sound. It wasn't coming from the car, and it certainly wasn't
the wind or the rain, and it wasn't thunder. It was a low, gut-
tural sound, of something massive that was straining to the
breaking point.

"Let's hurry and catch up with them before they get completely out of sight," Mrs. Peabody was saying.

"No!" said Nigel, now staring ahead at the bridge. "Stop!"

Lucy slammed on the brakes.

Ahead of them—as the taillights from the van climbed

up the road and out of sight on the opposite side—the bridge was collapsing. The storm-saturated foundations were giving way in the soft earth.

Their car fishtailed, slamming its occupants against one side and then the other. Finally it came to a stop.

They rolled down their windows and looked out—as the bridge surface in front of them collapsed and fell into the ravine with a wet, muddy roar.

"Well," said Nigel, after a short moment, "we can't go forward."

"No shit, Sherlock!" said Lucy, her breathing rapid and adrenaline-fueled.

Armstrong, positively cramped in the backseat, tried to stretch a kink out of his neck; for a short moment no one said anything. Then—

"Sorry," said Lucy to Nigel. "What now?"

Siger leaned forward between them and pointed at a narrow strip of ground that worked its way in switchbacks up the hill.

"We must take that side road," he said. "It's our only choice. If we just turn around, the road we were on just dead-ends. It doesn't go all the way around the island."

"More information that you Googled?" said Nigel.

"Well . . . yes," said Siger. "But anyway, the side road goes to the old Boy Scout camp. We can take shelter there."

"Are we allowed to do that?" said Mrs. Peabody. "McSweeney bought the camp, didn't he—to build his new estate? If we go to McSweeney's property, isn't that like investigating on our own and seeing evidence the other jurors won't see—and won't that cause a mistrial?"

"I'm not sure that I care," said Armstrong.

"I know I don't," said Bankstone.

"In any case," said Nigel. "the Scout camp is not the crime scene. And if the court is concerned about it, they can bring all the rest of the jurors out tomorrow to see it, too, when they come to rescue us."

Lucy put the car into gear, and they started up the hill. "We're going there regardless," she said. "If you haven't noticed—the windows on this bloody thing are leaking. I don't mind being inconvenienced to preserve our juristic integrity—but I'm not going to drown for it."

18

It was dusk, and nearly pitch-black from the storm. The car continued on the unlit road, passing the monastery ruins. Nigel looked through the window, and through the rain and darkness he glimpsed fragments of low walls and head-high stacks of rocks. Siger seemed to be paying attention to them, too.

The pools of water on the floorboards were now an inch deep and seeping into jurors' socks and between toes.

With each bump the car hit, more water sloshed. But the headlights shined a brief, hopeful glimpse on a structure at the far end of the road. Finally, a hundred yards up a steep dirt driveway that was in the process of washing away, they reached their destination. It was a two-story structure of dark, rough wood. There were no exterior lights. The jurors heard water pouring down somewhere from a roof gutter. It was still raining heavily, and they did not immediately jump out of the car.

"Perhaps it will look better in the daylight," said Mrs. Peabody.

"Do you suppose the door is unlocked?" said Lucy.

"It will be a simple task to pick it," said Siger.

He got out of the car and dashed through the rain onto the front porch. With the car's headlamps putting dim light on the door—and growing dimmer every moment—he took something out of his pocket and tinkered with the lock. He had it done within seconds. He shouted back at the car, "Got it!"

"Brilliant!" shouted Lucy.

"Elementary!" yelled Siger.

They entered the house—or at least started to—and then they all stopped short in the doorway.

"Let's hope someone left the electricity on," said Nigel. "If it was ever here at all."

He stepped just inside, groped along the rough, dusty wall for a light switch—and found one. Dim yellow lights came on. They were in the main hall of the Scouts' lodge. The light was from a decades-old sconce above the doorway, and an ancient cast-iron chandelier with 15-watt, flame-shaped bulbs that hung from the ceiling at the center of the room. Beneath that chandelier was a long, rectangular table of rough oak, with benches on either side.

The jurors all stood and looked, their clothes dripping puddles in the entryway. They could see what was directly in front of them, but not much else.

"I know jury duty isn't supposed to be a holiday," said Armstrong. "But I was looking forward to better accommodations than this."

"There's no way I'm spending the night in this dump," said Bankstone. "They need to get us the bloody hell out of here."

"Any port in a storm, my late husband used to say," said Mrs. Peabody. "Still, I think we should call someone and let them know where we are. Do you suppose there's a landline?"

"No," said Siger. "There isn't. There are no connections for one. I noticed that on the way in."

"And there's no cell signal on this island," said Bankstone.

"But we're only a mile from the hotel, and it's even less than that across to the mainland," said Mrs. Peabody. "Surely there is a way to communicate. Perhaps something more low-tech?"

"What, messenger pigeon?" said Bankstone. "Smoke signals? Or do you mean we should just try shouting?"

"You're already doing that," said Nigel. "I don't think it works."

There was an awkward silence.

"I'll wager there is no mini-bar," said Lucy, finally, "but do you suppose there is a kitchen?"

"Or a fireplace?" said Armstrong.

"That would be nice," said Mrs. Peabody. "Or, more urgently—a loo?"

"Yes, yes, and yes," said Siger.

They all looked at him.

"And you know this—how?" said Nigel.

"You see, but you do not observe," said Siger.

Nigel was familiar with this phrase. He was almost afraid to ask, but he did anyway. "Observe—what, exactly?"

"A stack of firewood to the side of the front porch. And a well with a pump connection and two sets of pipes leading into the house. What other purposes could they serve?"

"A fireplace?" said Mrs. Peabody, pointing. "Is that it there?"

It was in the shadows at the opposite wall. Siger went directly to it and found an old iron poker laying on the hearth. It took a moment—he knelt and looked closer, touching the remnants of someone's earlier attempt—and then he stood.

"Useless, I'm afraid. Rain has come in through the flue— it is all soaked."

There was another awkward moment—just discouraged sighs and shaking of heads—and then Mrs. Peabody spoke.

"Well then—if we can't have a fire, we'd better come up with something else," she said. "I think I'll go out and see if there's an emergency blanket or something in the boot of the car that could help us keep warm."

Mrs. Peabody turned to Lucy for the car keys, and then, as she moved toward the door, she took a flashlight out of her purse.

"You have a torch!" cried Siger.

"Why . . . yes, of course. I always carry one." She looked back at the other jurors. Both Nigel and Siger were staring at her. "Don't any of you?" she said.

"My dear woman," said Siger. "You have in your hand

the communication device you were wishing for earlier. We can flash a signal to the mainland!"

Now all the jurors crowded around.

"Oh," she said. "Oh. You're quite right. I knew there had to be some simple way. We can flash an S.O.S. Or perhaps even something more detailed, if any of you know Morse code."

"Of course," said Siger. "One never forgets the basics. It's just like typing."

"Thank god," said Bankstone. "They can send a helicopter and take us back to the hotel for a decent meal and clean beds."

"Hardly that," said Siger. "Our point in communicating is just the opposite."

"What do you mean?" said Bankstone.

"He means that it is much too dangerous to send a helicopter out in this storm," said Nigel. "And there's no point in sending an SUV, either, with the bridge down and the road washed away. We are safe here until morning, if not entirely comfortable, and what we need to do is let the authorities know that—so that they don't put a rescue party at risk, thinking that we might have been washed down into the ravine."

"Splendid," said Bankstone.

"But this flashlight is very small," said Nigel. "If we want any chance of it being seen, we'll have to take it out to the cliff."

"Naturally," said Siger. "Did I just hear you volunteer to go along?"

"Someone must," said Mrs. Peabody. "As my late husband used to say, one should never hike alone."

"Fair enough," said Nigel to Siger. "We'll help the ladies get what's useful out of the car—and then you and I will take a hike."

## 19

A short jaunt to the cliffs might have been a pleasant experience, on a sunny day in late spring or early fall, especially if it were in the company of Lucy, as opposed to Siger. But under the current circumstances, it was a bit of a slog. The rain alternated between heavy drizzle and gale-like sheets. Everything that was not rock had turned to mud, and each step was an opportunity to sprain an ankle or twist a knee.

The path began at the woodpile at the side of the house, where Siger tripped almost immediately, and went down on one knee. The man took a moment getting up, and he disgustedly tossed aside the chunk of old firewood that had been embedded in the mud and given him trouble.

There was a bit of residual light from the lodge, but beyond that the path was hardly distinguishable from the low brush and occasional stacks of rock ruins on either side of it. Siger led the way, using the flashlight at intervals, just every few yards or so.

"We mustn't dawdle," he said. "If the batteries wear out before we get there, we will have accomplished nothing."

They made it to the top of the slope. They both stopped and looked east—or at least Nigel hoped it was east—toward the mainland. For a moment they could see nothing below them but fog. It was still rising from the ground, as fast as the rain could dissipate it.

They took a breath. Siger instinctively reached for his pipe, but quickly abandoned the idea.

"There's something I've been meaning to ask you," said Nigel.

"Of course," said Siger.

"Ever since the first day of jury selection—you've been uttering things that are straight out of the Sherlock Holmes stories."

Siger nodded nonchalantly, as if Nigel's observation was both obvious and unimportant.

"Why?" said Nigel. "I mean, it's one thing to be a fan. It's something else to try to incorporate it into your daily life." Then Nigel thought about that for a moment longer, and added, "I should know. I've tried a bit of it myself. More than once."

Siger still had not answered the question. Instead, he peered into the distance and said, "This fog can't last. And I think it must already be clear a little farther down, at the cliff."

"Let me ask this another way," said Nigel. "How did you happen to become a juror?"

"I received a summons, of course."

"Yes, you would have to," said Nigel. "But precisely how did you receive it?"

Siger gave Nigel a long, suspicious look—and decided finally to answer. "It flew up against my feet," said Siger. "Completely unbidden. It would never have occurred to me to go looking for something like this. But one day several weeks ago, there it was, in the morning commuter rush—getting kicked by one hurried shoe after another, right down the stairs to my spot in the underground.

"The amazing thing about it was that it wasn't simply a discarded sheet of paper. And it wasn't crumpled up into a ball, either. Someone had actually taken the time to fold it into a little airplane before discarding it—and so with each kick down the steps, it took flight, just for a little—until it finally glided down directly in front of me."

Nigel winced slightly, and said, "So—you received your jury summons in the form of a paper airplane? At the Marylebone station?"

"Yes. It actually landed in my violin case—just like a tip."

Nigel stared, making the connection.

"I've heard the violin at that station. Many times. You're a busker. I've seen you playing, but you had a beard then."

"I've been many things. That was only the most recent of them. All on my way down, if you want to look at it that way, although it doesn't seem that way while you're doing it."

He took out his pipe again, and clearly wanted to light it, but didn't.

"I was in the third year of my medical residency. It was

going well enough, but I was exhausted, working twenty-four-hour shifts with less than six hours' sleep in between. I began to take amphetamines to stay awake and barbiturates to sleep in the few hours available. This was not sustainable, and the predictable happened: I crashed. In treating me after my breakdown, someone discovered that I'd been pilfering my meds from the hospital pharmacy.

"My residency was terminated. My dependency was not; it stayed with me as I failed at first one lesser job and another, until, eventually, I was as you saw and heard me at the Marylebone station.

"When I saw that summons, and who it was addressed to, it was more than just an official document from the Crown Court. It was a summons to a change.

"I thought that person could be me. Or at least what I could aspire to. Clean, and pure, and eminently, always, logical. But still human. Not an automaton, not a machine. But just dedicated to one thing, to understanding the order of things, without all the meanness of daily self-interest getting in the way.

"I wanted to do it. I had to do it.

"I knew there would be one problem, of course. What would happen when I showed up at the courthouse with a summons addressed to Sherlock Holmes? But then I read that the Crown would be trying to assemble multiple anonymous juries for some major trials. Anonymous, you see. That meant that I and my summons would need to pass scrutiny only once.

"It was cold, it was raining, and it was crowded, as you know, and the poor young lady tasked with admitting us at the alley door was overwhelmed and desperate to get us inside before we could all change our minds and run away. She had no time to worry about a surprising name. She assigned me a number and sent me in. And so there I was. Ready to be someone else. Or at least to be me in a different way."

Siger stopped talking now and stared out toward the mainland.

A fresh gust of wind blew through, and for an instant they saw it—in the distance, a speck of yellow light that had to be the pub on the mainland, and the faintest reflection on something that had to be the tidal bay in front of it.

Siger pointed the flashlight in the direction of that speck of light and sent three short flashes, two long ones, and then three more short.

"That's not S.O.S.," said Nigel.

"Right," said Siger. "If we needed rescue, I would have sent three long dashes in the middle, not just two. But we're merely checking in; so that was just an alert that I'm about to send a longer message. I think the light we are looking at is the exterior entry light of the pub. If they flick that one, or flash another back at us, we'll know we've made contact."

They both stared for a moment in the direction of the light in the distance. It did not change, and no other light appeared in response.

"Of course, it may take a few tries," said Siger, and he repeated the process. And then, after a short wait, he repeated it again.

Now the light in the distance seemed to vanish—then became visible again—and then vanish once more.

"Was that a response?" said Nigel. "Or did a cloud bank just roll in?"

"I don't know," said Siger. "But our battery is running low. So I'm sending the full message on the next clearing, whether they've seen us or not."

"What are you going to tell them? I mean, assuming someone is watching."

"Just that we're sheltering in place, and to please come get us at earliest convenience in the morning. Words to that effect."

Now the mist parted again, and Siger proceeded to send another, longer, series of dots and dashes. Nigel watched carefully—but he couldn't tell just exactly what words Siger was actually sending. His own knowledge of Morse code was just S.O.S., and nothing more.

Now the flashlight grew so weak that it was barely visible even right in front of their faces. And another cloud bank moved in and obscured the pub light once more.

"I'm afraid that's all we can do," said Siger. He flicked the switch on the flashlight a couple of times. It had gone out completely.

"Time to head back," he said. "I do hope they kept a light on for us; I counted our steps carefully along the way, so I don't think we'll take a wrong turn—but it could be a challenge getting back in the dark even so."

And it was. There was indeed a bit of residual light visible at the kitchen doorway, but they couldn't see their own feet as they walked back.

"Blast!" said Siger as they approached the woodpile outside the kitchen. He had tripped once again, just as he had on the way out.

As he got up and tried to brush the mud off his knees, the kitchen door opened. Mrs. Peabody greeted them.

"Ah. There you are. We were just about to send out a patrol to rescue you. I mean, if we had one."

Nigel thought this was probably an exaggeration on Mrs. Peabody's part; Bankstone and Armstrong, both seated at the table, did not seem all that concerned. Lucy was by the fireplace, on her knees, peering in at the damp ash. Siger walked over to her immediately.

"All waterlogged, as you see," he said, preparing to kneel next to her and look in as well.

"Yes," said Lucy. She got to her feet, and came over to join the others at the table. "You're quite right."

"We've been busy taking inventory while you were out," said Mrs. Peabody, perhaps just a little more cheerfully than was warranted. "And what we have is four bedrooms upstairs, and a loo in the corridor. The beds are just wooden platforms—no mattresses. We did, amazingly, find a stack of old woolen blankets, but it's a close call whether to use them, given what might be living in them after all these years. And the loo has no paper. There's a wall lamp in each bedroom, and even a bulb or two, but the ones in the stairwell and corridor are out, and there are no replacements. There's a cast-iron stove, but no food to cook on it. We took a quick look in the lower kitchen cupboards and the only potential dinner item was a four-legged one with a tail, which skittered at first, but then got on its hind legs and made us understand that the food chain here is in dispute. So now we've all pooled our food resources, with what we happened to have with us and what we found in the car—and there it all is, right there on the table."

Nigel went to the table and saw the following:

One package of wine gums.

One opened and half-consumed roll of Mentos.

One unopened sleeve of Hobnob's chocolate-covered oatmeal biscuits.

A tiny plastic container of spearmint Tic Tacs, which looked as though it had been in someone's purse or pocket for too long a time.

"That's it?" said Nigel. "That's our entire communal collection of food?"

"The Tic Tacs are mine," said Bankstone. "I'm willing to trade one Tic Tac for one Mentos, but only from the inside of the package—I don't want the Mentos on the end, which has been exposed to god knows what."

Armstrong glared at Bankstone. "I brought the Mentos," he said. "But I'm not trading a Mentos for one bloody Tic Tac. I'll only trade for a Hobnob's, and I'm willing to trade two for one if need be."

Siger shrugged and said, "I have some pipe tobacco, if that will help."

"You see, we are just about to politely divvy things up in civilized fashion," said Mrs. Peabody to Nigel and Siger. "It's good that you got here in time, or I would have eaten your share, whatever that turns out to be."

Mrs. Peabody had excellent organizational skills from her years of marriage, and she continued. "With all of us here now, I think we get two Hobnob's biscuits each. I brought them, so that's how we're going to do it. If there's an odd one left over, it's mine. I had my fill of wine gums on the bus, so you may distribute those evenly among you. The remaining items you can fight over as you like. Now, as to the rooming arrangements—I suppose two of us will have to share, and select roommates in the proper way."

"Yes," said Nigel, after just a moment's thought. "Alphabetically by first name."

Lucy smiled slightly.

"No," said Mrs. Peabody, "by gender, of course."

"Of course," said Lucy. "I'm sure that's what he meant. You and I will share."

There was another awkward pause. Bankstone stared at the wine gums.

"Well," said Mrs. Peabody. "Now that's settled—I, for one, have had quite enough of this day. If all of you don't mind, I'm off to whatever sort of bed awaits me until the morning."

She was clutching her purse tightly as she went. Nigel wondered if this meant she had an unacknowledged granola bar in it that she was eager to consume without sharing.

Or perhaps not. Perhaps she was as generous as she seemed.

"That makes sense to me, too," said Armstrong. "Good night." Armstrong went up the stairs.

Bankstone muttered something unintelligible, took his share of biscuits and a couple of extra wine gums as well, and he went upstairs, too.

Now Nigel waited, but said nothing. He did want a couple

of biscuits, but that wasn't what he wanted most. He was looking for an opportunity to be generous with the right person.

If only Siger would take a silent hint and go away.

Lucy said nothing, and waited.

"So," said Siger, "just the three of us then. Shall we have a seat? I think this day has given us much to consider."

Lucy gave a little sigh, and said, "It feels quite late to me. I think I'll just go on up and dream of the wonderful complimentary breakfast all the other jurors will probably be getting in the hotel in the morning."

She glanced at Nigel, smiled in a way he could not decipher with any certainty, and went up the stairs.

Siger seemed dumbfounded. "No one wants to talk anything over?" he said, as they both watched her exit.

"Amazing, isn't it?" said Nigel.

Siger shook his head, then took his pipe and tobacco out of his pocket. "Do you mind if I smoke?" he said.

"Not at all," said Nigel. "Especially as I'm turning in as well." Nigel started toward the stairs.

"It's not smoking to be smoking, you know. It's the ritual. It helps me think."

"Ah," said Nigel. "Well. Good luck with that."

## 20

Nigel couldn't sleep.

It was partly because the bed had no mattress, just wooden slats, and the room was chilly, and the wool blanket smelled dank and mildewy. And at first it was also because he kept replaying the moment when the cloth of the insurance agent's shirt had slipped from his grasp.

But there was nothing else Nigel could have done, and there was never any possibility that the two inches of cloth that he had grabbed would have supported the man's one-hundred-and-eighty-pound weight. He knew that.

Still, it was difficult to sleep. He needed to think of something else.

Lucy came to mind. Again.

He knew she was sleeping in one of the other rooms on the same floor. He wasn't sure which one; it might even be the one right next door. At this very moment, she might be sliding out of her rain-wet clothes and into—well, into whatever. Nigel contemplated that for a moment.

And now he really couldn't sleep. But it wouldn't do to lie awake thinking about her, either.

What else could he think about?

Something came to mind immediately.

Bangers and mash. Fish-and-chips, with vinegar and a pint of Harp. Blood pudding and baked beans.

Perhaps a granola bar.

Anything at all would do. He was desperately hungry, and now that it occurred to him, that thought crowded out all the others, at least for a moment.

And then it occurred to him that if he did find anything to eat, he could invite Lucy to share it with him. It would give him an excuse to knock on her door—if he could find the right room. Probably her roommate was already asleep, but surely Lucy was still awake. At least, she would be if she was having the same sorts of thoughts as Nigel.

And if she were, then of course, anything could happen.

Providing a meal to a woman in the hope of having sex. Looking at it in that light, Nigel supposed that Lois might be right after all. Perhaps jury duty was indeed like a dating agency.

In any case, his incentive was now twice, or maybe even three times, what it was just a moment ago. He got off his uncomfortable bed, opened the door into the corridor, and looked out.

No one. All was quiet—except for the rain on the roof.

And it was dark. But not so dark that he wouldn't be able to make his way downstairs to the kitchen and pantry. Their initial investigation of the cupboards had surely been done with the haste of people who were as damp and cold as they were hungry.

Perhaps they had overlooked something canned and sodium-nitrated, tucked away in an upper corner, lasting forever, and destined for just this moment.

Canned Spam, perhaps. Spinach. SpaghettiOs. Anything.

Nigel shut his door carefully and slowly—but with a prolonged squeak even so—and then proceeded down the corridor to the stairs.

The stairs squeaked, too, especially the last step—but by that point, the fantasy that there might be something to eat had become so strong that he didn't care if he woke anyone. He stumbled through the dark onto the main floor and found the light switch again. Then he went to the three rows of cupboards that served as the pantry.

It was unlikely that anyone had fully explored the two narrow and dusty cupboards in the back corner of the top row. To do that—to get to those back recesses—required a bit of climbing. Nigel put one foot on a lower shelf, got a knee up onto the wood countertop, and reached into the back of the top cupboard, blindly groping, and hoping that he did not find a rodent or a trap for one.

His fingertips found deep, ancient dust—and then something else.

It didn't bite him, it didn't snap shut on his fingers, and it was metallic. All good signs. He boldly seized on it and withdrew it from the cupboard. He wiped the dust off, and could hardly believe what he was seeing in the dim light.

It was Spam. Just as he had imagined there might be! Rarely had any fantasy been so specifically, precisely realized. The only thing that could make it more complete would be if—

"What are you doing?"

Nigel turned. It was Lucy.

"Did you find food?"

It was both a question and an accusation, and Nigel hesitated. Something deep in his id—or somewhere—wanted to respond with, "Shall we have sex?"—but of course, that approach wouldn't work, and in any case he was much too civilized to try it—at least in exactly that way.

"Maybe," he said after a moment.

She stared. "Is that Spam?"

"Yes," said Nigel, like a child into the cookie jar.

"And were you going to just take that back to your room and eat it all yourself?"

This remark might have been teasing, but Nigel wasn't sure. "Well, no," he said. "My fantasy—I mean, my idea— was I'd find you. Maybe clear all the gunk out of the fireplace, strike some rocks together to get a spark, and build a little fire somehow. Sit in front of it. So we could cook. The Spam, I mean."

"Oh," she said. "Oh. Well. That's all right then."

"Unfortunately, it's missing its little tab key at the bottom. Which is probably why it got tossed into the corner and has been sitting around for the past decade or two."

"That's too bad." She sighed. "I suppose even Spam expires someday."

"I think I read once that it's supposed to last virtually

forever, like a very deep attraction. Or maybe that was Marmite."

There was a pause, and Nigel worried that an opportunity might be about to slip away. "So," he said, with the awkwardness of someone stating the obvious, "you were looking for food as well?"

"Actually, no," she said. "I heard the stairs squeak, and I came out hoping it was you. There's something I want to show you."

She was wearing a thin cotton shirt, slightly damp, her nipples were alert, either from the cold or not, and she was wearing spandex pants—Nigel wasn't sure whether they were properly regarded as pajamas, or yoga gear, or what—that adhered tightly to her skin. Nigel—still standing precariously on the counter—watched her slide one hand inside the waistband on her right hip.

Nigel slipped from the counter, dropping the can of Spam, and banging his knee on the way down.

"Are you all right?" she said.

"Yes, of course," said Nigel, resisting the impulse to rub his knee. "Sorry, didn't mean to interrupt," he said. "You were about to show me—I mean, you were saying?"

"Oh, right," she said. "But let me help you . . ."

Nigel was on the floor with the can of Spam, and she knelt to help him, which was excellent, he thought, because clearly he required no actual assistance with anything—but now they heard something—a new squeak on the stairs— and they both looked up.

"What are you two up to?"

It was Mrs. Peabody. She was wearing a flannel nightdress

and carrying a keychain-size LED flashlight, even smaller than the one she had provided earlier, and she aimed it at the can of Spam.

"Spam," said Nigel. "Although from a previous decade. I've been looking for an opener, but no success."

"Oh, I don't know. From the look of things, I think you're doing all right so far. My late husband used to say, there's no such thing as gratuitous assistance."

"Quite the cynic, your late husband," said Lucy, standing.

"Yes, he was. It came from his line of work, I suppose," said Mrs. Peabody, still shining a light on the can of Spam. "Have you checked all the cupboards thoroughly for something we might use to open it?"

"Open what?" said a new voice.

They all turned. It was Bankstone.

"We have Spam," said Nigel. "But nothing to open it with."

"I'm starving," said Bankstone. "Perhaps someone should check the woodpile outside for an axe or a sharp rock or something?"

"Any Boy Scout who left an axe outside to rust should lose one of his badges," said Nigel.

"Well, that's no reason not to check," said Mrs. Peabody. "As my late husband used to say, desperate times, desperate—"

"I'll go check," said Lucy quickly, interrupting. "It will only take a moment."

"I'll go with you," said Nigel, stepping forward—but she put her hands lightly on his chest and pushed him back.

"No, no, you did your part, you hunted up the Spam, and practically broke your knee doing it," she said. "I'll be right back." Lucy opened the door and quickly stepped out into the gale, slamming the door behind her.

"Brave girl," said Mrs. Peabody.

"Yes," said Nigel.

"Or an unusually hungry one, to go into that just for a little Spam," said Mrs. Peabody.

Yes, thought Nigel, to risk a soaking and pneumonia just for that little can of processed pork, she must be either very hungry—or quite selfless. And it was rather ungallant to let her do it alone.

He waited perhaps three seconds, and then said, "Something might be wrong. I'm going after her."

"No good deed goes unpunished," said Mrs. Peabody. "As my late husband used to—"

Nigel strode forward and opened the door, and then immediately stopped. There was Lucy, standing right in front of him, holding an axe, limply, in one hand. She said nothing. She seemed dazed, more than just a little confused—and quite fragile, with her shirt soaked and her brown hair in wet string-lets.

"Oh good," said Mrs. Peabody, standing behind Nigel. "You found a can opener."

"What?" said Lucy. Then she looked at the axe in her hand. "Oh. Yes." She stepped inside.

Nigel took off his coat and wrapped it over her back and shoulders; he guided her over to the wooden bench. She sat, dropping the axe to the floor. It made a wet impression there, which was mostly water, but not entirely.

Mrs. Peabody got down on the floor and looked closely at the joint between the axe handle and its blade. "There's blood on this axe," she said.

"Yes," said Lucy, in a numb voice. "It was in his head. The axe, I mean. Well, the blood, too, of course. At an earlier time."

Mrs. Peabody, Bankstone, and Nigel were all speechless for a short moment. Then—

"Whose . . . head?" said Nigel.

"Mr. Armstrong's."

Nigel ran outside to look. The gale was still blowing. Laying amidst a scattering of fallen fire logs, unmoving, the blood from his head beginning to dissipate in the pelting rain, was the body of Mr. Armstrong.

Nigel knelt by the man's head. The pupils were fixed. Nigel looked up—Mrs. Peabody had now come outside, and stood in the rain, staring down.

And now Lucy came out again as well.

"Where is Bankstone?" said Nigel.

"He went upstairs to get Mr. Siger to help," said Lucy.

"Let's not wait," said Nigel. "If you can each get one leg?" Nigel put his hands under the man's shoulders. "On three."

Nigel counted to three and then, with some difficulty, they managed to lift the body off the ground. They staggered to the doorway, which opened just in time, with Bankstone on the other side. They brought Armstrong's body in and laid him out on the long wooden dining table.

"Where's Siger?" said Nigel.

"I couldn't find him," said Bankstone. "He's not in his room."

Mrs. Peabody checked Armstrong's body for a pulse. "He's gone," she said. "There's nothing to be done." Then she added, "I hope we didn't do the wrong thing bringing him in. You're not supposed to move a body from a crime scene."

Nigel looked at her.

"I mean, assuming a crime is what it was," she added. "And not an accident."

"How else does one get an axe in one's head?" said Bankstone.

"It's odd, isn't it?" said Mrs. Peabody. "We presume he was killed before we all came downstairs, which would have meant he was out in the rain for at least twenty minutes. So how could it be that blood was still on the axe? Shouldn't it have all washed away?"

"Not necessarily," said Nigel. "The blood we saw was just from the narrow joint between the axe blade and the handle. The rain has been intermittent. If he was struck, say, half an hour ago, the blood could have congealed in that narrow space, and it would take some time for the rain to wash it all away."

"You have steely nerves for a woman," said Bankstone to Lucy. "You discovered the body of a man recently killed, but you did not scream."

"Didn't I?" said Lucy. "Odd. I felt that I did. But if none of you heard it, I suppose the storm must have drowned it out." Then she added, "I'll be glad to scream now, if you like."

"She was in shock, the poor dear," said Mrs. Peabody. "Anyway, what in the world are you suggesting?"

"I'm not suggesting anything," said Bankstone. "I just want to know what happened."

"Perhaps it was an accident after all?" said Mrs. Peabody, though without much conviction. "There were many logs scattered about, freshly I think, given that some were soaked only on one side but not the other. Perhaps the axe was on the top of the pile, and poor Mr. Armstrong was pulling a log out of the bottom of the pile, and the axe fell on the back of his head, and then one of the logs fell on the axe, driving it in farther, and—well, it's not impossible, you needn't all look at me that way. Stranger things have happened. Anyway, perhaps it was no one's fault."

"I think we've had too many accidents," said Bankstone. "Let's count through them. First there was the woman who fell down the stairs and broke her hip."

"She was using her phone on slippery stairs in a crowd that was in a hurry," said Lucy. "Not all that surprising she would fall."

"Yes, but then there were the two jurors who got food poisoning in the cafeteria. And then the insurance salesman fell to his death from the cliff."

"He was more than a little tipsy," said Nigel. "I think he had several pints at the pub."

"So did I," said Bankstone, "but I didn't fall off the cliff. The point is, this is too many accidents. Too many coincidences."

"My late husband didn't believe in coincidences," said Mrs. Peabody.

"Was there anything your late husband did believe in?" said Lucy.

Mrs. Peabody thought about it. "Yes. Two pints at the end of the day. Sometimes three."

"We're ignoring the obvious," said Bankstone.

"Which is?" said Nigel.

"Jury selection by attrition. Someone is trying to get the juror of their choice onto the jury—to control the verdict or at a minimum hang the jury—and they're killing people to make it happen."

"But except for Mr. Siger—wherever he is—all of the original alternates for this trial are right here, in this room," said Lucy. "They are us. Or were. Mrs. Peabody and I are primaries now."

"Yes," said Bankstone, "But I've been a primary from the beginning. And right now, that's making me nervous."

"So you think," said Lucy, "that one of us is the person that someone wants on the jury?"

"Yes," said Bankstone. "One or more."

"And you think the unfortunate accidents won't stop until that person or persons is next in line to be on the jury?"

"Yes."

"So," said Mrs. Peabody, "I suppose the question is, how many of the rest of us have to be eliminated to get the right one or ones onto the jury? And who are the right ones?"

Nigel said nothing. He didn't like where this was heading. Also, there was another important question, and it was not a happy thought—but no point in suggesting it just yet.

And then it got suggested anyway.

"Wait a moment," said Bankstone. He began to pace back and forth. "Wait a moment. There's something else. Think about it. There was no one around the first juror when she fell down the stairs but other jurors. There was no one around when the insurance salesman fell from the cliffs except other jurors—specifically, all of us. And there's no one here at the cabin now except the four of us."

"You mean the five of us," said Mrs. Peabody.

"Right," said Lucy, looking at Bankstone. "You didn't include Mr. Siger."

They all looked at each other in new and unnerving ways.

"Right then," said Mrs. Peabody. "So it's one of us that is killing the others in order to get onto the regular panel. Is that what we think?"

"It's the only explanation," said Bankstone. "One of us is guilty—and if we're all going to make it through the night—we need to figure out which one."

For a moment they all stood in the center of the room and regarded each other warily. Then Mrs. Peabody spoke again, and very much as though she knew what she was talking about.

"Historically, there are a number of ways to go about this," she said. "Though I'm not sure I would recommend any of them."

"What ways?" said Lucy.

"Well, if you go back far enough, there's trial by force of arms. Two individuals have a grievance, they both pick up their broadswords—or the biggest sticks they can find, depending on which century you were in—and go at it. Winner is in the right; loser, if he survives, was in the wrong."

"But this is not a one-to-one dispute," said Bankstone.

"You're right, it isn't," said Mrs. Peabody. "And I don't

suggest that method anyway, since I'm not physically the biggest and strongest among us. But there have been other approaches. There was trial by magical ordeal. You throw someone in a well; if he or she floats, then he or she has the devil inside, and so needs to be burned or hanged from a special kind of tree. Of course, if the accused is innocent, then they sink. Problem solved, either way."

"No," said Lucy. "We're not doing that, either."

"Well then," said Mrs. Peabody, "there's the continental approach—trial by inquisitorial prosecution. One of us would be the judge, and there'd be a prosecutor, and a defense, of a sort, and after they've both made their cases, the judge decides, all by himself. Now personally, I would like that one, but only if I get to be the judge. I'm qualified, you know, because my late husband was one."

"No disrespect," said Nigel, "but let's not do that one, either."

"All right. We're narrowing it down. Of course there's also the approach of conviction by popular acclaim," said Mrs. Peabody. "Like the trial-by-drowning approach, it has the advantage of being easy and quick. We all just point accusingly and yell at each other for a bit, and then we have a vote, and whoever gets the most negative votes is kicked off the island. So to speak. Personally, I think that approach is garbage."

"So do I," said Nigel.

"Me, too," said Lucy.

"All right then. Our only remaining alternative is quite obvious, as I suppose our friend Mr. Siger would say—assuming he's not lying somewhere with an axe in his head—"

"Or wielding one," said Bankstone.

"The remaining alternative is this," said Mrs. Peabody. "We gather all the available facts, we make any deductions that are warranted—and then we submit them to a jury to decide."

"You mean we have a trial," said Nigel.

"Yes, I think you can call it that."

"For whom?" said Nigel.

"Each of us in turn, I suppose."

"And what do we do if we find one of us guilty?" said Lucy.

"First things first," said Bankstone. "Let's get on with it and figure out who it is. Everyone sit down at the table."

There was a general hesitation—no one had yet come to any conclusion that Bankstone was the boss—but no one had any better suggestions.

So each of them took a seat on one of the benches on either side of the dining table.

For a moment—with the body of Mr. Armstrong laying on the center of the table between them all—no one spoke.

"Talk about awkward," said Lucy. "We shouldn't have put Mr. Armstrong on the table. Especially if we're all going to get together for breakfast in the morning. I mean, if we ever get the Spam open."

"My guess is we aren't going to like each other very much by morning anyway," said Mrs. Peabody. "I mean, presuming of course that we all survive that long."

"Well, I'm not sitting next to his face," said Lucy. "It's . . . morbid."

"Let's move the bench to the other end of the room, by

the fireplace," said Mrs. Peabody. "And then we'll take turns. One person will sit there on the stool, and the others will sit there on the bench and listen, and another person will ask the questions. When we're done with one person on the stool, we'll all change places and go to the next."

"What about Mr. Siger?" said Lucy.

"We can worry about him later," said Bankstone. "If he decided to go for a walk or something in this storm, that's his own problem."

"I don't think she meant that in the sense of is he in trouble and do we have to go rescue him or something," said Mrs. Peabody.

Yes, she did, thought Nigel.

"Well, actually, that is what I meant," said Lucy.

"Oh. Sorry," said Mrs. Peabody. "But what I'm wondering is—what if it's Mr. Siger that has been—well—killing us? We don't want to convict him in absentia, of course, but if we can determine that it was him, then we'll know that all we have to do to protect ourselves is keep him out until help arrives."

"All right then," said Bankstone. "Let's figure out if it's him, and if we decide it isn't him, then we'll decide which of us it is. I'll be the one that asks the questions. I'm the prosecutor."

"No," said Nigel. "We'll take turns at that."

They were standing eye to eye. Bankstone blinked.

"All right," he said. "We'll take turns."

"Yes, yes, of course," said Mrs. Peabody. "I'm sure that's what you meant. You can begin, Mr. Bankstone."

With that dispensation, Bankstone took a deep breath,

squared his shoulders, and stood up very straight. "Now then," he said. "We know the means. It was this axe, right here." Bankstone picked the tool up by its handle and displayed it for everyone to see.

"You shouldn't have done that," said Nigel.

"Done what?"

"Picked up the axe. Now your fingerprints are on it."

"What's your point?"

"We might have been able to take fingerprints from the axe, with a little charcoal dust from the fireplace. But now you've handled it, so your fingerprints being on it will no longer tell us anything."

"Bloody hell, I'm not a suspect!"

"Now, be fair," said Mrs. Peabody. "We're all suspects."

"The axe won't be conclusive anyway," said Nigel. "Not by itself. It was out in the rain, and most of us touched it when we moved the body."

"Fine," said Bankstone. He began to pace, still holding the axe in one hand. "Then let's do motive."

He rubbed his chin for a moment, and then he said, "It seems to me that Mr. Siger was behaving a little oddly from the very beginning."

"How so?" said Nigel.

"Anyone who has any sense at all tries to get out of jury duty—but that bloke seemed to be going out of his way to get on it!"

"Well, actually," said Mrs. Peabody. "I think your premise is wrong. Of all of us, the only one who I think made an actual effort to avoid jury duty was you. All of the rest of us were willing."

"Well, in my book, that makes you all suspects. Willing is only one step from eager, and eager is suspicious. But there's more that points to Siger."

"Like what?" said Nigel.

"He spent a lot of time analyzing other jurors in the canteen. That's exactly what someone would do if their purpose in being there was to stack the jury somehow. He was assessing everyone, to determine how they would likely vote, so he'd know who to bump off and who to leave on."

"That's a stretch," said Nigel.

"No," said Mrs. Peabody, thoughtfully. "No, I don't think so. It rather makes sense to me. Are we ready to take a vote?"

"No, wait—don't answer yet," said Bankstone. "There's more." Something in the way he phrased that caused them all to look at him with great anticipation. Bankstone continued, "Doesn't it seem odd to any of you that Siger has known so much about the island? And what about the questions that he asked during the trial? And talk about cold-blooded—have you ever met anyone who knows so little about sports? So little about the celebrities on reality telly?"

"Weirdness is not evidence," said Nigel.

"All right then—there's the axe, which was the means; and the motive, which is jury nobbling; and the opportunity— did he have that? The answer is yes!" Bankstone turned with a great flourish, clearly wanting to point at someone— but of course Siger wasn't there to point at.

But Mrs. Peabody was nodding in agreement. Even Lucy looked as though perhaps she was being swayed. She glanced at Nigel.

Nigel stood. "Your entire premise is faulty," he said to

Bankstone. "You've presented no motive for Siger to have wanted to influence the jury, but even if he had one, there is no way he could have planned any of this. None of the events associated with the island—starting with the insurance salesman's plunge from the cliff and including the axing of Armstrong—could have happened unless we came to the island. And there was no plan to do that when the trial began. Siger could not have known that it would happen, and he did not do anything to make it happen. Coming here was the judge's decision."

"Bloody fool of a judge," said Bankstone. But then he thought about it. "Now wait a moment," he said. "It wasn't the judge that wanted to do this—it was one of us! It was the question from the jury that made it happen. And that question was not from Siger, that question was from . . . from . . . from you!"

Bankstone was pointing right at Nigel, and now continued with great energy. "Were you or were you not alone in this kitchen just thirty minutes ago?"

"Well . . . yes, but—"

"And your only excuse for having come down here was to find a can of Spam?"

"Well . . . yes."

Bankstone turned to the other jurors. "A can of Spam!" he said, with an inflection that said they should be as incredulous as he was. Then he turned back to Nigel.

"You seriously expect these jurors to believe that you came down to the kitchen in the dead of night for nothing but a can of Spam?"

"Yes," said Nigel. "Pretty much. Spam and whatever else

it might lead to. But I really don't think you're giving Spam the credit it deserves. When thinly sliced and properly fried, so that it is nice and crispy around the edges—"

"That's quite enough about the preparation of Spam, thank you. Now let us back up just a bit. Let us think back, to the first day of the trial. Do you remember that?"

"Of course."

"Then let me ask you—were you in the hallway when primary juror number seven fell down the stairs?"

"Yes."

"And in the canteen, did you warn Lucy here not to get the white sauce for the pasta?"

"Well, yes."

"And it was indeed your question that resulted in this site visit and our trip to this accursed island, was it not?"

"Yes."

"And on the cliff, you were the last to touch the insurance salesman before he fell?"

"I . . . think so."

"And you were downstairs alone this evening before the body of Mr. Armstrong was discovered?"

"Well . . . yes."

"Aha! Fellow jurors, I submit that Mr. Heath here is the planted juror and is the one who has been bumping us off. It's time to take a vote."

"Sit down, young man," said Mrs. Peabody. "This is not an election and it's not a popularity contest. It's a trial." Mrs. Peabody said this with great authority, and for a moment Bankstone looked just a little sheepish.

He sat down. "All right, all right, as you say."

"Thank you," said Mrs. Peabody. "Now then—does any-one have anything else to say?"

Apparently no one did—Nigel looked from one to an-other, and no one had any help to offer.

"I didn't do it!" said Nigel.

"Yes, of course, you are entitled to your denial," said Mrs. Peabody. "So—now it is time to take a vote. What say you all?"

"Guilty," said Bankstone quickly.

"I vote guilty, too," said Mrs. Peabody.

Now Mrs. Peabody looked at Lucy. Lucy hesitated. Nigel looked at her expectantly, and she looked back—but still she hesitated.

"I abstain," she said.

"You can't abstain!" said Mrs. Peabody, sounding quite exasperated now. "We have to reach a decision!"

Lucy looked away from Nigel. She looked at each of the other people in the room, one at a time, then up at the ceiling—and then she finally looked back at Nigel again, and she sighed. "Guilty," she said.

Nigel stared at her, open-mouthed. He could not believe what he'd just heard.

"Right, then," said Bankstone. "Let's tie him up."

"I don't think so," said Nigel, standing.

"No one agreed to anything about tying anyone up!" said Lucy.

"Well, that's the whole point, isn't it?" said Bankstone. "How else are we going to get any sleep? If we don't tie him, he'll wait until we're all asleep and then sneak up and hit us with an axe!"

"But what if he's not the real killer?" said Lucy.

"She has a point," said Nigel.

"We just now found him guilty, did we not?" said Mrs. Peabody.

"Yes, but what if we're wrong? What if the real killer is one of the rest of us? If we tie him and leave him down here by himself, he'll be at the killer's mercy."

"Well . . . that's a risk I'm willing to take," said Bankstone. "Anyway, we've reached a verdict. It's time to pass sentence."

Bankstone turned toward Mrs. Peabody. "What do you say?"

"Personally, I just hope someone comes to rescue us soon. Another hour of this, and we're all going to just degenerate into something like out of *Lord of the Flies*."

"Oh, that can't happen," said Lucy. "We're English, after all." Then she thought about it. "Oh. Right. I see your point."

"So let's all keep calm. I think I know just what will help," said Mrs. Peabody. "I want you all to just sit right here very quietly, and don't do anything rash, while I go into the kitchen for a few moments."

"But what—" began Bankstone.

"Shh," said Mrs. Peabody. "I said quietly."

Mrs. Peabody picked up her purse and went into the kitchen. Nigel, curious, half-stood to follow. She shook her finger at him. "Sit."

Nigel sat.

It took several minutes. While they waited, Bankstone glared suspiciously just once in Nigel's direction, but then looked away. Nigel looked at Lucy, trying to understand why she had voted the way she did, but she just gave a sheepish smile in return, then turned up her nose and looked straight ahead at nothing.

After a few minutes and some metallic banging noises— and then a scent that was unmistakable—Mrs. Peabody emerged from the kitchen.

"Here we are," she said. She had a paper cup in each hand, both of them full of something hot, by the way she was carrying them. "Of course we've no milk at all. But one can't get more civilized than this."

"You have Earl Grey tea?" said Bankstone, sniffing the air.

"You had matches?" said Nigel.

"Yes and yes," said Mrs. Peabody. "I saved it all for when we would need it most. I think that appears to be now." She handed the first cup to Lucy. "Here you are, dear," she said. "No *Lord of the Flies* for us."

She gave the second one to Bankstone. "You've been try-ing ever so hard, I know," she said. "A spot of tea will chirp you right up. Or even you out. Or whatever. As my late hus-band used to say, good for what ails you."

She looked at Nigel and said, "Now don't think I've for-gotten you. I'll be right back." She went back to the kitchen and then returned with two more cups, one of her own, and one for Nigel.

"Here, dear, nice and warm. Very relaxing. We didn't mean to upset you."

Mrs. Peabody looked about the room, at each of them holding their cups of tea. "Well, go on," she said, "sip up."

Everyone obliged.

"Now then," said Mrs. Peabody. "Clearly there's only one thing to do, and that's for all of us to just stay right here in the same room until help arrives. That way, the perpetrator, whoever it is, can't take any of the rest of us unawares."

"Oh, that can't work," said Bankstone.

"Why not?" said Lucy.

"Because . . . because . . . well, what about going to the loo?"

"We'll go in pairs, of course," said Mrs. Peabody. "We ladies do it all the time, you gents will just have to get used to the routine. And we'll take turns sleeping—just two at a time—so that we always have at least two people awake at any one time."

Bankstone looked from one juror to the next.

"Suits me," said Nigel.

"All right," said Bankstone, finally relenting. "I apologize for thinking about going out to the car and perhaps finding a nice roll of duct tape in the boot. But tell me this—who sleeps first and who stays awake, and in what combinations?"

It was a complicated question, and much discussion followed, during which Bankstone, still apologetic, went into the kitchen himself and made them all some more tea. Nigel hoped that somehow the sleeping arrangements would end up with just himself and Lucy awake and together, and everyone else asleep or otherwise not around.

But as important as that outcome was, and even with the second servings of tea, he was finding it hard to stay awake at all. Even though he had gotten a reasonably full sleep

the night before and had ordered only one pint at the pub—
and despite everything that had been and was still going
on—he found himself nodding off.

He raised his head up and looked about. He didn't see
Bankstone. Or Mrs. Peabody. There was a noise in the
kitchen that might have been them, but Nigel was fading too
fast to get up and look.

He did, however, see Lucy.

She was right next to him, sitting on the floor. Perhaps
she was a little wobbly herself. Or perhaps not—now she
was pushing herself off the ground, about to stand. The
pants on her right hip slid down a bit as she did this, and
now, finally, Nigel got a full look at the tattoo.

It was a blue crown, with three stylized blue lions beneath
it, and for good measure, beneath that were what looked like
crossed swords, only they weren't swords—they were cricket
bats. It was the logo of the England cricket team. Nigel
blinked and wondered if he was just imagining things.

And then he was out like a light.

## 21

Nigel dreamed that he was still back in Los Angeles, and that Mara was not next to him only because she had just gotten up, and all he had to do to find her again was to simply get up himself.

And then his conscious mind began to recover. He opened his eyes. He knew where he was now. Under other circumstances, he would have just gone back to sleep and tried to recover the dream.

But now he was groggily awake, with a dull headache, and he was just aware enough to know that current circumstances were such that he should not go back to sleep. On the floor next to him he saw the paper cup from which he'd been drinking tea. He saw Lucy's paper cup as well—but not Lucy herself.

He got to his feet, felt nauseous, and leaned on one end of the rough oak table.

He saw Mrs. Peabody. She was sitting on the bench, head down on the table, asleep. Snoring slightly. And there was an empty paper teacup next to her as well. And there was something odd about the table. It took a moment, and then he realized—the body of Mr. Armstrong was gone.

Nigel staggered into the kitchen and almost slipped, catching himself just in time on the edge of the stove. He looked down to see why he had slipped—and he saw water beginning to accumulate on the floor. In his still drowsy state, he supposed it might have spilled when Mrs. Peabody made the tea. Something in the back of his mind told him there was too much water on the floor for that, but at the moment he didn't really care. What he wanted to know about was the tea itself.

The sides of the stove were still warm. There was an old iron kettle, in which Mrs. Peabody must have heated the water for the tea. Nigel sniffed at it, but did not detect anything but the residual scent of the Earl Gray.

Then he looked in the lower cabinet. There was an old coffee can that had served as a waste receptacle. In that can was the paper wrapper that had contained the tea bags.

But on the cupboard floor near the can—not in it—were more than half a dozen of the little foil packages that typically contain allergy capsules.

Like Mrs. Peabody's allergy capsules. The kind that double as sleep aids.

Nigel thought for a moment about what that meant.

And then he heard a sound from outside the kitchen door. He opened it and stepped outside. The rain had tapered off, at least for the moment. But the wind hadn't; it was blowing the clouds in a steady stream overhead, with occasional gaps, and right now, through one of those gaps, there was enough moonlight to see the woodpile clearly—and Lucy standing near it, with one of the fire logs in her hand.

She looked a bit muddy. The wind was blowing her hair, and her cheeks were red—either from the wind, or from sudden adrenaline, or both.

"Now we know which of us is the heavier sleeper," said Lucy. "And also which of us snores."

"I wasn't awake when you were asleep," said Nigel. "So we haven't had a real test of that. Yet."

"I'm so sorry I voted you guilty," said Lucy. "But I was suspicious of Mr. Bankstone, and I thought it was the only way I could figure out what he was all about. Of course I wouldn't have let anything happen to you. And then when I dozed off, and I woke up and he was gone—well, I thought it best to just leave you and Mrs. Peabody as you were for a bit. For myself, I guess I'm lucky that I never really liked Earl Gray tea; I only took a few sips."

"Bankstone was gone when you woke up?"

"Yes. And so was Mr. Armstrong's body, as I'm sure you noticed. But there's something here I want to show you."

"I was hoping we'd get to that," said Nigel.

"Well, you have to come closer."

Nigel walked up next to her, very close, and he looked, and waited.

"What are you looking at?" she said.

"What you're going to show me," he said, fully expecting that she was going to show him the cricket team tattoo that he had glimpsed before losing consciousness—and that then she was going to confess to something. He just didn't know exactly what that would be.

"Well, it's down there," she said. She was pointing at her feet. "You'll have to get down on your hands and knees to see it, I think. Like I just did."

Nigel got down on the ground to look. He hoped she wasn't going to hit him over the head with the fire log, but he was still too groggy to worry about it very much.

He looked at the wet ground. At the completely flat surface that seemed out of place. He pushed the water and mud out of the way.

"See it?" she said.

"It's a door," said Nigel. "A trapdoor."

"Yes," she said.

Nigel cleared more of the mud away, and in the process realized that he wasn't the only person to do this recently— the mud was heavy and thick at the edges, but thin, fresh, and watery on the wooden surface of the door.

It wasn't old wood. It was recent; simple plywood used in modern construction.

"We're not the first ones to discover this," said Lucy.

"No, we're not."

"Can you lift it?"

Nigel felt around the edges. There was no handle— whoever had put this in place had not intended it for frequent use—but there were hinges. And opposite those, Nigel found a crease.

He lifted the door.

Water and thin mud immediately ran into the opening.

And out of the opening came a scent of tobacco smoke. Pipe tobacco.

"Oh, I'm so glad," said Lucy. "This means Mr. Siger is alive, don't you think? That he's gone below into a tunnel?"

"I hope that's what it means," said Nigel. "That is, I hope it's a tunnel and not just a grave, and that he's in it somewhere. But without any light, it's bloody difficult to tell."

"I know, but I think it's a tunnel—and you'll think so, too, when I show you what I found in the fireplace."

This was an awful lot of good news in quick succession— Siger might be alive, the lovely woman with the cricket tattoo was not a juror murderer who wanted to hit him over the head, and she didn't want to go down into the pitch black tunnel without a light, either.

But the rain had started up again, and it was getting heavier by the second. Nigel stood, put the trap door back in place, and brushed the mud and water off his knees.

"Show me," he said.

Nigel followed Lucy back into the lodge. They sloshed through more than an inch of water on the kitchen floor, and now Nigel could see the source of it—or two of many probable sources, actually. A steady stream was pouring down from the ceiling at one of the wall joints, and an ambitious drip had begun right in the center. Which had to mean that on the second floor above them, water had already pooled heavily.

Nigel vaguely hoped that someone had homeowner's insurance, but at the moment there were other concerns. He followed Lucy into the main room.

Mrs. Peabody, still at the table, raised her head slightly as they entered, and muttered, "Don't track mud in, children."

Then her head was down and she was asleep again.

Nigel followed Lucy to the fireplace. She got down on her hands and knees in front of it. She reached into the cold, wet ashes and pulled out a clump of burned paper.

There were only fragments left—someone's attempt to burn the sheets had been almost completely successful—but she detached one of the fragments, about two inches square, and showed it to Nigel.

The writing was in a woman's hand—flowing, elegant, and imaginative. There were only a few words still visible, but they were enough: Until then, my love. Marlie.

"Do you see?" said Lucy.

"I think so," said Nigel.

"These are the love letters that Mrs. McSweeney wrote. They do exist. Liam McSweeney did see them. It must have happened on their holiday here before she was killed. Perhaps she intentionally showed the letters to him, to make him understand that she could have a life of her own. Or perhaps she brought them here to destroy them, because she was ending the affair, and he found the ashes, just as we did. Or perhaps he discovered the letters and burned them himself in a rage. Those are all possibilities. But these are the letters, and the tunnel outside is how he got between here and the mainland more quickly than anyone could imagine, without being seen crossing the water."

"The monks' tunnel," said Nigel.

"Yes." Lucy lifted up her feet as she said that. Her shoes were soaked. "Oh."

They both stopped paying attention to the fireplace. They looked about them. There was water everywhere.

Mrs. Peabody, still slumped at the table, lifted her head now and looked at the floor and said, "I asked you not to track mud in, children." And then she raised her head, fully awake.

"Oh, dear," she said.

"There's this thing called situational awareness," said Nigel. "I think we all need to get better at it."

The water was inches deep across the floor. They could hear a major cascade in the kitchen, but they didn't need to go look—it was coming down in streams right in front of them, and there was a sound of groaning timbers from the floor above.

"Time to go," said Nigel.

They all three ran outside. The rain and wind were as strong as ever, but staying in the lodge, with all the water pouring onto the ceiling, and saturating the foundation and soggy earth all around—was not an option.

The sedan was still there in front, with water and mud swirling on the tires.

"Do you still have the keys?" said Nigel.

"Looking," said Lucy.

"Bankstone got out somehow," said Nigel. "But how? He wouldn't have tried to walk out in this, and the Fiat is still here. So how did he leave?"

"The tunnel?" said Lucy.

"For his sake, I hope not," said Nigel. "That's the last place I would want to be in a flood."

Nigel looked at the ground immediately in front of the lodge, in a small area protected by the eaves. He knelt down for a closer look.

"I've found the keys," said Lucy.

"Then let's go, shall we?" said Mrs. Peabody.

Nigel stared at the mud directly under the eave. "This is a tire track," he said. "Not ours. Someone else's. And it's a huge tire. I've never seen anything like it."

"So someone came and picked Mr. Bankstone up—and took Mr. Armstrong's body—and left all of us behind?" said Mrs. Peabody.

"It would seem so," said Nigel. "It reminds me a lot of my partying days at university."

"Sometimes it is good to be separated from the herd, and sometimes not," said Lucy. "But if it were an official rescue team, they would not have left anyone alone here. We'd all be sitting on each other's laps if necessary. And what is their possible destination? The bridge is out, and they know it—so they cannot be taking the road in that direction."

"They can't be heading to the hotel by land," said Nigel. "So they're either trying to get to McSweeney's estate—or they're heading toward the sea."

"I'm not sure I would like that sort of deliverance," said Mrs. Peabody.

Nigel nodded. "A trained amphibious team could get through that surf line in a craft made for that purpose. But untrained city dwellers in a small boat? Not a chance. Not until the surf calms down."

"Then let's catch up with them," said Lucy. "Whichever way they went."

22

The starter motor in the sedan whirred—but no ignition.

Lucy turned the key again. Same result.

"How do you feel about doing a push start?" she said to Nigel.

"Crank it again," said Nigel. "Longer. If it doesn't work this time, we'll end up just floating down the hill. That would not be good."

She tried again. And this time the engine turned. It belched out gray smoke, and it kept running. Lucy put the car in gear, and they started down what remained of the driveway.

They reached the main road. To the right was the washed-out bridge. They turned left, with the water runoff getting worse—but there was nowhere else to go.

"It shouldn't be more than half a mile," said Nigel. "We should see one fork that goes up the hill toward McSweeney's estate—and another that goes down to his beach and boathouse."

MICHAEL ROBERTSON

Lucy ground the gears and managed to get the car into second.

"I think our theory about jury selection through attrition is wrong," said Nigel, as the car pushed along through the mud. "I don't think this has been about getting one or more specific jurors onto the primary panel. At least not once we reached the island and realized how unlikely McSweeney's alibi is. One or two jurors, no matter how persuasive, would not be able to sway all the rest of us and get an acquittal."

"What's it about then?"

"It's just about getting a mistrial. Nothing more. Someone is trying to reduce the total number of jurors, so that there won't be a verdict in this trial. What comes after, when McSweeney gets retried, they must not be concerned about."

"But what good does that do McSweeney, if he just has to face a new trial, with more evidence against him?" said Mrs. Peabody.

"Not much," said Nigel. "That's my point. I don't doubt that McSweeney would do anything he could to get an acquittal. But there's something else at work here, too."

Now Lucy reduced their speed to a crawl. "There's the fork," she said. "Which way?"

They peered through the windows. To the left, one fork went up the hill toward the estate, and to the right, the other fork led toward the cliffs and the beach. The estate wasn't visible; it was beyond the rise, and if it had any lights on, they didn't show.

But it made no difference. That road was gone.

"It's washed out," said Lucy. "We can't get up there."

"No," said Nigel. "And I don't think anyone else could, either, in the last twenty minutes, no matter what they're driving."

"Then I guess we're going to the beach," said Lucy, and they took the fork to the right.

It wasn't far. They went perhaps a hundred yards, rounded a curve—and below them, at the end of the access road, they saw a small boathouse—and the sea.

"I don't see a boat," said Mrs. Peabody.

"No," said Nigel. "McSweeney doesn't have one. But he's supposed to have his own sea tractor."

"There," said Lucy, pointing beyond the boathouse. "Just inside that rocky point on the right!"

Nigel looked. Just inside the surfline, rolling and listing with each white cap, was the sea tractor. It looked like a sort of seagoing cage, not really a watercraft at all, at least not intended to be. It had no hull. It had tires that were over three feet high and two feet wide, and the base of it, on which people were supposed to stand, was perhaps six feet off the ground—but in the high tide and surf, that was not nearly enough. The sides of it were almost completely open, with nothing but a couple of brightly painted horizontal boards to keep its occupants in, and nothing whatsoever to keep the water out.

And there were two occupants—a tall figure at the steering control toward the middle of the platform—and another figure hanging desperately onto the side rails as the vehicle pitched with each swell. And there was a bulky object of some kind laying on the platform.

As they were watching, the vehicle tipped at a 30-degree

angle, and the object on the platform slid off and into the surf.

"That can't be good," said Nigel.

Lucy put the car into gear and drove down the access road until they reached the sand. Mrs. Peabody stayed in the car. Nigel and Lucy got out and ran to the little boathouse. It wasn't much; no bigger than a walk-in closet, with just some beach towels, a couple of ropes, and rescue buoys.

They stood in the boathouse and watched the sea tractor. But only for a moment.

"What in hell are they doing?" said Nigel. "They're running just inside the breakers. They'll tip."

And just as he said it, the sea tractor leaned radically on its side again with an incoming wave, and the figure standing at the rail was suddenly no longer there.

Nigel and Lucy stared out at the surf line until they saw movement—arms, head, and shoulders, struggling against the white water of the breaking waves.

"There," said Nigel.

"I see him," said Lucy.

Now the sea tractor was visible again—and Nigel could see that it had not, in fact, capsized at all. It had listed when they first saw it—but now it had recovered—and there was still a figure standing at the helm.

Nigel expected that the vehicle would be turning now, and coming back toward the person who had gone overboard. But no. It wasn't doing that. It was turning away, heading toward the far end of the point. It was rounding that point now.

"Can you swim?" said Nigel.

"Like a fish," said Lucy. "And I took the training. I'm even better than Daisy."

Nigel didn't ask who Daisy was. He handed one rescue buoy to Lucy and he took the other, and they both went into the surf.

# 23

It was almost dawn.

Nigel and Lucy and Mrs. Peabody all huddled in the boathouse, wrapped in all the available beach towels except one.

That one was draped over the body of Mr. Bankstone.

"You were very brave to try," said Mrs. Peabody. "It was just too late."

Nigel and Lucy just nodded. They were too exhausted from their rescue efforts to speak.

"I'm glad you know it wasn't me that drugged you," said Mrs. Peabody. "I've never had any complaints about my Earl Grey before."

"It had to be Bankstone," said Nigel. "I saw the allergy pill wrappers that he just tossed under the counter. We know you would never have done that, Mrs. Peabody. You are tidy. You would have carefully disposed of them in the coffee can."

Lucy turned to Mrs. Peabody and said, "It actually was rather good tea. And I don't even like Earl Grey."

"Thank you, dear."

"Bankstone was taking no chances," said Nigel. "He was sure one of us was the murderer, but he didn't know which— so he drugged us all."

Now Mrs. Peabody suddenly stood. "Look!" she said. "Look! Out there! We're saved!" She was pointing out to sea, just beyond the promontory.

Nigel and Lucy, as exhausted as they were, got up and looked, too.

It was a pontoon boat—the emergency services rescue boat. Just now crossing the white crests of the surf line, disappearing for an instant behind a swell but then appearing again as surely as Big Ben chimes the hour. Sunlight was breaking through the clouds, striking the boat, which gleamed in response.

It was glorious.

Standing at the front, leaning forward as if doing so would propel them all the faster, was the judge, his white hair blowing in wispy strands.

"Yes," said Lucy, wiping away sea water from her eyes, "I believe we are."

## 24

An hour and a half later, morning sunlight glistened on the residual raindrops still clinging to the signboard of the Running Monk pub. The waves had subsided, and so had the wind and tide that had generated them.

The few remaining surfers were no longer at the tidal inlet at all, but well to the south, catching the last storm swells before they could disappear entirely.

There were no pub patron cars in the car park. The entrance had been cordoned off with yellow tape and portable barricades; two police cars were parked there, and another was directly in front of the pub. A car next to that one was unmarked—except for the New Scotland Yard parking sticker in the corner of the windshield.

There was a medical emergency vehicle as well, just now pulling away from the car park, but with no siren—it was too late for that. It was followed by the same chartered bus, with darkened windows, that had delivered the jurors originally.

The constables at the car park entrance allowed those vehicles to depart, but then quickly closed the barricade again, ahead of the first news van that had now appeared at the far end of the road.

The pub door opened, and Maggie stepped out to hand a cup of coffee to Constable Bailey, stationed at the door. He nodded gratefully; she smiled in return. And then, before going back inside, she paused to look out toward the island. A police helicopter was moving slowly across the interior of the island, and the sea tractor—its blue railing glinting in the sun—was turning away from the island shore and coming back toward the pub—with, apparently, no one but the driver on board.

Maggie shook her head sadly and went back into the pub. On a normal late morning, Maggie would have been heating up Heinz beans and tomatoes and other essentials that the locals liked in their English breakfast. On this morning, no locals without official business had been allowed to get in—but there were hungry people even so, and she went into the kitchen to prepare their plates.

She had already lit the wood in the fireplace. She had done that as soon as the coast guard boat with three soaked jurors had come up and docked. Those jurors were now wrapped in gray wool blankets and seated on the bench in front of the fire.

Standing at the bar were two coast guard crew members, filling out something on a clipboard. Seated at a table between the bar and the fireplace were all the officers of the McSweeney court—Mr. Justice Allen, Mr. Slattery, Mr. Langdon, the steward Ms. Sreenivasan, and the bailiff,

Mr. Walker, who sat calm but alert, looking from the jurors to the front door and then back again. The judge sat with his head down in his hands. He would look up occasionally at the jurors drying out in front of the fire and then bury his head in his hands again.

Maggie suspected that he desperately wanted a pint, but she brought him the coffee he had asked for instead. "Please serve them first," said the judge, nodding toward Nigel, Lucy, and Mrs. Peabody, all seated by the fire. "I arrived here yesterday with fourteen jurors. Now I have eleven. At the rate bad things seem to be happening to them, I'd like to at least make sure these three don't die of malnourishment."

"They'll eat first," said Maggie, "but you take this right now." She put the coffee down in front of him and went back to the kitchen.

The front door opened and two chief inspectors and one sergeant entered. The judge raised his head, but he didn't speak to the men who'd just arrived. He was too tired, and aside from that, it was not really his place to do so. This would be a new investigation, and he must stay out of it. He nodded toward the blanketed jurors in front of the fireplace and then turned back to his coffee.

Chief Inspector Wembley from London, in the well-worn gray suit, paused to let the local chief inspector, who had clearly worn his best to this occasion, to approach the jurors first. Chief Inspector Rutledge moved toward them, and when none of the exhausted jurors immediately raised their heads, he stepped between the nearest of them and the warming fire.

Mrs. Peabody looked up at him and said, "Have you located Mr. Siger?"

"No," said the inspector.

"Then rescue services is still searching?"

"Of course."

Nigel looked up and followed that exchange—but said nothing.

"Now then," said the inspector, "I am Chief Inspector Rutledge of the Devon West district. With me are Inspector . . . Chief Inspector . . . Wembley from Scotland Yard and Sergeant—"

"Sergeant Thackeray, sir," said the sergeant.

The inspector nodded, and continued. "We know you must all be quite tired. But we have some questions, if you don't mind."

"We don't mind," said Lucy. "Provided that, as Mrs. Peabody said, this isn't slowing the search for Mr. Siger. And also provided that you don't stand between us and the fire."

"Quite so," said Mrs. Peabody, looking up at the inspector. "You are being rude, young man. And if you cause me to get a worse pneumonia than I'm already likely to get, I'll sue you."

The local inspector took a step back.

Inspector Wembley smiled slightly and helped Sergeant Thackeray drag some chairs over from a nearby table and set them up on the periphery.

"Where do you want us to start?" said Nigel.

"From the beginning would do," said Inspector Rutledge.

Nigel hesitated and looked at Wembley for clarification.

"Let's start with when you last saw Mr. Siger alive," said Wembley. "And how the three of you came to be at that beach."

"We all took refuge at the Scout camp," said Nigel. "Mr. Siger and I went out to the bluff to send a signal to the mainland, and then we returned to the camp. We all tried to turn in for the night, but eventually we all ended up downstairs in the kitchen. Except Mr. Siger. He was missing. And except Mr. Armstrong, whom we discovered dead at the woodpile."

"So none of you saw or heard anything of Mr. Siger after that?"

"No," said Lucy.

"No," said Mrs. Peabody.

Nigel scratched the back of his neck, looked Wembley directly in the eye—and just shook his head.

Wembley studied Nigel for a moment, then continued. "Who found the body of Mr. Armstrong?" said Wembley.

"I did," said Lucy. "I came back in and told the others."

"And then we brought the body in and put it on the table," said Mrs. Peabody. "And then we all gathered around—the four of us—and had a delightful argument about what was going on and who was doing it. And then—"

The local inspector put up his hand to stop her. "Not getting along well, then, the lot of you?" he said.

"Oh," said Mrs. Peabody. She paused and thought about why he was asking, and she said, "Well, nothing like *that*, of course."

"Like what?" said the local inspector.

Mrs. Peabody looked to Lucy and Nigel for help.

"It was just a conversation," offered Nigel. "It did not get out of hand."

Wembley looked hard at Nigel for a moment, and then said, to all of them, "In any of the conversations among you—did you hear anything that might make you think that anyone might want to harm any of the jurors?"

Nigel and Lucy and Mrs. Peabody all looked at each other. Nigel shrugged. So did Lucy. Then—

"Well," said Mrs. Peabody. "The insurance salesman fellow was an insurance salesman, so of course there's that. But I can't for the life of me think of any reason anyone would want to harm Mr. Armstrong. And as for Mr. Siger— well, he struck me as an odd duck, but nothing anyone would get upset about."

"Other than the fact that he was one of us," said Lucy. "A juror. On this trial."

"Well, yes, there's that, of course," said Mrs. Peabody. "But anyway—what happened next after Mr. Armstrong died is that we drank tea and fell asleep, but it wasn't the fault of my tea. And when we woke up, Mr. Bankstone was gone—and so was the body of Mr. Armstrong."

Wembley looked at Nigel for confirmation, who nodded.

"And then," said Nigel, "we found unusual tire tracks outside the door. We followed those tire tracks, and they led us down to the beach. Right down to the surf line. We saw the sea tractor, and we saw Mr. Bankstone get dumped into the surf. We were too late to save him."

"Did you see the driver?"

"No," said Nigel. "Not close enough to recognize."

"It had to be someone Bankstone trusted though, don't

you think?" said Lucy. "Otherwise, he would never have gone along."

"You got a good look at the tracks?"

"Yes," said Nigel.

"Range Rover? Hummer? Could you tell?"

"Larger," said Nigel. "Much larger. And with a clearance of at least two feet."

Maggie, behind the bar, glanced over when Nigel said that. She stopped what she was doing, went to the front door, and looked out—and then she came over to the group seated in front of the fire.

"The sea tractor is coming across now," she said. "It should be out front in about five minutes."

"The sea tractor?" said Wembley. He was the only one of the group who had never seen it before, and so the only one who had to ask. Maggie pointed at the photo of it that hung on the wall behind the bar. "Ah," said Wembley. "The sea tractor."

Maggie went back to the kitchen. She returned a few moments later with three full breakfast plates. She put one down in front of each of the jurors.

The front door opened, a blast of cold wind blew in, and Bert with it. The bailiff and the barristers all turned to look. So did the judge. And so did the chief inspectors from both jurisdictions, the sergeant, and all three living and present jurors.

"Whew," said Bert to Maggie, as he walked directly up to the bar. "That's still not a pleasant trip in this weather, I don't mind telling you."

Bert suddenly turned his head in the other direction,

pulled a checkered flannel cloth out of his coat pocket, and sneezed into it.

"Gesundheit," said Maggie.

"Thank you," said Bert.

Maggie nodded in the direction of the police officials. Bert turned toward them and then came directly to their table. His attitude was almost touching in its eagerness. "I've been up and down the coast on the near side of the island three times," said Bert. "I've been clear around the whole thing once, and I explored the creeks on both sides, and it was no easy thing, what with the heavy mud runoff. Never seen anything like it. But I found nothing. I'm sorry, lads. But there's just no trace of the juror that's still missing. Not a trace at all."

No one said anything in response. Suddenly Bert heard the silence, and was unnerved by it. "What?" said Bert.

"Sit down and join us for a moment," said Wembley.

Nigel watched Bert's face, and saw his expression turn from eager self-congratulation to suspicious fear.

"What?" said Bert again.

"Just sit down, Bert." said Chief Inspector Rutledge.

Bert very cautiously took a seat.

Rutledge leaned in toward Bert and looked him right in the eye, which was the local inspector's very best move, and said, "Bert, we've got one juror suspiciously dead from the Scout camp. We've got one suspiciously dead from the surf. And we've got one still missing. Suspiciously. If that juror is still alive, and you know anything about it, the time for you to tell us about it is right now."

"But I don't, guv! I looked all over the island for him, just as I said. I didn't make him go missing, guv. And I didn't do anything to the others, either!"

"You're a betting man, aren't you, Bert?"

"I . . . yes, I play the lottery. I do."

"Like your sports, too, don't you?"

"Why, sure. Manchester United is my team."

"That's football," said Rutledge.

"Um . . . yes."

"We're talking cricket here."

"All right then," said Bert.

"Got any bets down on cricket?"

"No."

"What?" said Rutledge. "Do you mean to tell me you aren't heavily into the bookmakers on the upcoming cricket championship?"

"Well, no, guv, I'm not. That would be a fool's game now, wouldn't it? Given how up in the air everything is?"

"Don't play with me, Bert."

"I'm not, guv. I wouldn't."

Rutledge sighed and sat back.

Wembley stood and tapped Rutledge on the shoulder.

"Don't go anywhere, Bert," said Rutledge. "I still want to talk to you."

"I won't, guv. I promise."

The two chief inspectors walked several paces away, toward the back of the pub, and then Wembley spoke in a low voice. "It doesn't matter whether Bert personally has a bet on the match," he said. "His bookie could already be heavily invested himself on odds that he set before McSweeney was even arrested. So if Bert is heavily in debt to a bookie, and the bookie wants to influence the match by cocking up the jury, then the bookie's motive becomes Bert's motive, get me?"

"Of course. I knew that. I'm just taking my time about it. Sneaking up on him, as it were. We haven't even read him his rights yet."

"All right then. It's your jurisdiction."

"Right. It is."

The two inspectors returned and sat down in front of Bert again. "Here's the situation, Bert," said Rutledge. "You've been seen drinking pints and otherwise fraternizing with known bookies. You've acknowledged placing bets, and we'll know soon enough just how deeply in debt you are. So that's motive. We know the sea tractor was the only vehicle for miles around that could have gotten up to that camp during the storm. We know the tracks from that vehicle led from the Scout camp right down to the shore where this Mr. Bankstone drowned in the surf. And we know that you are the only person authorized to drive the sea tractor. And I think you know what that means."

"But I couldn't have done it!" cried Bert. "I was here at the pub. Maggie can tell you that. And the sea tractor was there at the island. So how could I possibly get there?"

"Ah," said Rutledge. "That's where you thought you were being clever, all right. But not clever enough, lad. You've been talking for years about there being a secret monks' tunnel from here to the island. We believe you found it. That's how you got to the island."

"But there is no tunnel," said Bert. "I never found it!"

"So you say now, Bert. But I'm a betting man myself, and

I'll wager that you did. And if you found it, so can we. We'll get the entire archeological team of the British Museum out here if we have to, but we'll find it. And when we find the tunnel, we'll find your fingerprints, and your shoe prints, and maybe even some sweaty DNA of yours on something. And then we'll have you dead to rights."

Bert's distress eased a bit now—and began to sound something like defiance. "Guv, I didn't do it. But if you think I did, and finding that tunnel is what you're basing it on, I'm not worried. Because that tunnel ain't there. So you better just start looking for somebody else to pin this on, because you'll never put it on me."

"So you say," said Rutledge. He glared at Bert, seeming to mull the situation over. "Tell you what, Bert," said the inspector, finally. "I'm going to let you stew on this for a bit. Give you a chance to get out in front of it, so you don't make things worse for yourself. I've got no grudge against you personally, and I know where to find you. You come clean, I'll cut you every break I can."

"I didn't do it."

"You think it over, Bert, just like I said. I'll be in touch."

Chief Inspector Rutledge went toward the exit now, and Wembley accompanied him. Rutledge stopped at the door. "This is how we do things here locally, Inspector Wembley," he said, so loudly that even Nigel and the other jurors, seated by the fire, heard him clearly. "We have our ways."

"And good ways they are," said Wembley.

"Glad to hear you say so, Wembley. Cheers."

Rutledge exited, and Wembley returned to sit near the jurors at the fireplace.

All eyes were now on Bert. The entire pub was silent for a moment. Then Maggie spoke from behind the bar. "This is a rough go, Bert," she said. "But you stay right there. I'm going to serve you up the biggest breakfast you've ever had, just in case you end up—well, I mean, just in case."

The judge turned to Mr. Walker. "Go outside and check with emergency services. Make sure they're still looking. Make sure they're still treating this as a search and rescue. If you get any sense they're doing otherwise, let them know they'll answer to me."

The bailiff nodded and then walked toward the exit with a stride that clearly said he was ready to knock heads if need be. And just in case anyone had doubts about it, he actually did bump into Bert on the way out. And he didn't even bother to excuse himself.

Wembley was studying Nigel closely. "You know, Heath," said Wembley after a moment, "you'll get kicked off the jury when I tell the judge you summoned me out here. He can even find you in contempt for that if he wants to."

Nigel looked back at Wembley.

"This jury is done anyway," said Nigel. "But are you saying one of us contacted you?"

"A telegram, actually. Don't get many of those anymore. It said 'Come at once,' and it was signed simply 'A McSweeney trial juror.' The local inspector got one last night as well. I thought it had to have come from you."

"It wasn't me," said Nigel.

"And then when we got here, we found a note."

"That said what?"

Wembley shook his head.

"If you really don't know," he said. "I guess I'd better not tell you."

"What did the note say?" asked Nigel again.

Wembley shook his head again, and sat back in his chair. "Wait for it, then," he said. "Wait for it."

## 25

On the golf course behind the pub, the rain had begun to ease—but it was still flowing in rivulets wherever it could find the slightest slope, and forming water hazards in places where water hazards had never been seen before or wanted at all.

One of those ambitious hazards was beginning to form right now at the border between the golf course and the pub's back lawn. A brief gap in the clouds allowed the sunlight to hit it—just as there was a major disturbance in the two-inch-deep water.

The disturbance was from underneath. And suddenly all the water in that one particular little pool began to rush and gurgle through a brand new opening, as rapidly as if someone had pulled a plug.

Immediately after, a human noise, like cursing in a cavern, came from below. "Damn!"

Now, with the little pool drained, a rectangular patch of mud and green grass suddenly raised itself at a 45-degree angle—and then flopped completely back on the ground behind it, as precisely as if on a hinge.

Which it was.

A head with a cap on it appeared in the opening, and gray eyes peeked over the grassy edge. Then narrow shoulders appeared as well, and then hands gripped the sides of the opening—and then Siger pulled himself halfway out of the tunnel.

His cap and shoulders were soaked and muddy from the drained pool. But beyond that, he looked no worse for wear. He looked quickly about to confirm again that no one was watching. Then he climbed out completely, stood on the soggy ground, and calmly took a moment to survey his surroundings.

He already had a reasonable sense of the distance between the tunnel opening and the pub, because he had emerged from the tunnel once before. But that had been several hours earlier, in the dark of night, and in the pelting rain.

Now he wanted to make sure in daylight of the hiding place that he would use.

And he desperately needed a moment to get the kinks out of his back and legs. Apparently ninth-century monks were not very tall. If they ever had it in mind to cause lower back pain for possible Nordic pursuers, that tunnel would certainly have accomplished that goal.

Siger stretched his back and looked to the west, where the clouds had lifted and the island was visible once more, freshly green and damp, with the hotel glistening in white contrast. The tide was ebbing, and patches of sand were appearing where waves had been crashing earlier.

To the south—just about fifty yards or so—was the back of the pub, and beyond that the car park. Just a few yards to the north was the golf course, the fence that separated it from the pub land, and, just on the other side of the fence, a tailored, grass-covered mound next to a sand trap.

Siger looked down at the concealed trapdoor that he had forced open. It was not quite so concealed now—but with the water and mud and generally disturbed landscape all around, it could still be reasonably restored to its disguise— at least until someone got near enough for close inspection.

So he put the cover back in place. He pushed the mud and loose grass and water around a bit to help out. Then he stooped under the loose wire fence, walked several yards onto the golf course, and positioned himself in the sand trap behind the grassy mound.

The ground was still wet, of course, but it couldn't be helped. He'd sat on worse surfaces in his life. He sat down, and got out his pipe, but didn't light it—smoke would rise up and be visible. So he kept the pipe unlit, and waited.

And waited. He was beginning to grow impatient. Perhaps this was not such a good idea after all. Perhaps it was a capital mistake. Or if not a capital mistake, at least an inconvenient one, as far as he personally was concerned. Perhaps his message had not gotten through and the chill in the ground was aching his bones for no good purpose at all.

He shifted position uneasily. His knees were cramped. His lower back hurt. His butt was cold. He wanted to stand up.

And then he heard it.

The splash of footsteps. Heavy. Long strides. But now growing nearer, and now becoming tentative.

Now very near—and now stopped.

Siger waited—just one moment longer—and then he heard the sound he was waiting for.

The squeak of the metal trapdoor.

Siger jumped up, aching joints notwithstanding, and turned, ready for a face-to-face confrontation.

Looking back at him, slack-jawed in surprise, was Mr. Walker, the bailiff. In one hand he was grasping the opened trapdoor to the tunnel—and in the other hand he held Bert's checkered flannel handkerchief—with all the DNA on it that Bert had so recently deposited.

Mr. Walker straightened to his full height. Siger, not at all short himself, but no match for the man he was staring at, stood very still, saying nothing but giving no ground.

Finally the bailiff let out a heavy sigh. "I knew it," he said.

"Yes," said Siger quietly. "It's not something I say often—but sometimes you should trust your instincts."

Mr. Walker let go of the DNA evidence he had hoped to plant. He looked over his shoulder. Behind him, coming out of the back door of the pub, were Wembley and Rutledge—and behind them, with a look of disappointment and dismay so clear that it broadcast all the way across the lawn, was the judge.

"I knew it had to be a trap," said Mr. Walker, looking about lamely as they all gathered around. "I knew it had to be. And I came anyway."

The judge just stared, sadly. He could say nothing, and finally Chief Inspector Rutledge just escorted Mr. Walker back into the pub.

Nigel walked up next to Wembley, Sergeant Thackeray,

and Slattery the prosecutor, as they stood by the tunnel entrance. Siger was still standing there as well. He looked at Nigel, and then at the officials, and he waved off the opportunity to explain, and began to light his pipe instead. Nigel turned to Wembley and the others.

"This tunnel is how Mr. Walker got to the sea tractor on the island, and then returned to the mainland after, without anyone knowing," said Nigel. "If things had gone according to plan, he wouldn't have had to do it. But I don't think things went according to plan.

"And the tunnel is also how McSweeney got across from the island so quickly and without being seen. He discovered the entrance on the island after he began prepping the Scout camp for construction. He didn't tell anyone at the time, of course—the historical conservancy would have stopped him from building there if they'd known about it. In any case, now that we know how he got back and forth, I expect you can use this to destroy his alibi in the retrial."

"You're right," said Wembley. "I think we've got him now."

Slattery shook his head. "Not with the way everyone feels about McSweeney. We'll give it a go, of course. But they've poked holes in our motive before, and they will do so again."

"That can't be so, can it?" said Sergeant Thackeray. "What about the letters? They found her love letters, didn't they? And that shows motive, doesn't it?"

"It might have, sergeant," said the prosecutor. "It just might have. But between the Scout lodge washing away, and the jurors going into the surf and losing everything they had in their pockets—well, there's nothing left of the letters. But we'll do our best. We'll get him if we can."

Nigel, Wembley, and Slattery walked back into the pub. The sergeant remained behind, staring disgustedly down at the tunnel entrance. Siger remained behind as well, puffing on his pipe, and now he walked up to the sergeant.

"Perhaps you should tell them," said Siger.

"Tell them what?"

Siger sighed and consolingly put a hand on the sergeant's shoulder. "That's not up to me to say," said Siger, before walking on. "I'm just a juror."

Inside the pub, Constable Bailey entered to help Inspector Rutledge take Mr. Walker into custody. But no assistance was needed. The bailiff stood calmly at the door waiting for them—and as he waited, he tried to explain it to the judge.

"I've been gambling a bit, sir," said Mr. Walker. "Well, a lot, actually. And losing. And not to the legitimate bookies, either, but to the types that were here yesterday. They gave me a chance to erase it all. But it wasn't supposed to go this way."

Nigel, Mrs. Peabody, and Lucy walked over to him now. "How was it supposed to go?" said Nigel. The bailiff took a breath, and then he told them.

"I was in debt to the gambling syndicate, but I wasn't the only one. On the first day of jury selection, they had seven jurors in the assembly hall who they had already bought or blackmailed. When the random selections were made, two of those seven were put into the general selection pool. That should have been enough. One of those two got himself booted out by wearing an England cricket team jersey. I think he got cold feet and did it on purpose. But we still had the insurance salesman, and he was a very persuasive bloke.

He alone might have been able to sway the whole jury to an acquittal—and if he couldn't get that for us, at least he would hang the jury. It was my job to get him from the alternate pool into the primary twelve, and I managed it—I just gave the first woman a little nudge on the stairs, nothing serious, mind you, just enough of an injury to remove her from the pool. And then I got two more primary jurors out by adding a little something to their pasta sauce as they went through the lunch queue. And that was enough to move our insurance salesman ringer into position. But then he got himself drunk and stood too far out on the rocks. That wasn't my fault. Act of god, so to speak. But that meant we no longer had anyone on the jury we could control. And it wasn't going well, especially when jurors started poking holes in the alibi. There might have been a conviction. The scum that hold my debt wouldn't take that chance. So they—I—did the only thing we could—reduce the number of jurors to the point that there would have to be a mistrial."

"You killed two people!" said Mrs. Peabody.

"Only jurors," said the bailiff. And at that moment, Constable Bailey put the plastic ties on his wrists, and escorted him out the door.

Mrs. Peabody said to the judge, "Does he think that makes it all right?"

The judge put a hand on her shoulder. "Don't take it personally. You may have wondered why I am so against juror fraternizing? Mr. Walker had a bad experience last year, and I'm afraid he's been going downhill ever since. A young female juror passed her phone number to him in a note. They went out, even though we have rules against it. And when he was suspended temporarily for doing that, she dumped him. Apparently her initial attraction toward him had something to do with the uniform."

"Oh. Well . . . I suppose I can understand that," said Mrs. Peabody. "He did look quite sharp in it."

## 26

On Monday morning at the Old Bailey, the McSweeney jurors gathered in the Court 13 corridor once more.

Mr. Justice Allen had given some consideration to not bringing them together in the courtroom again at all. So much had transpired that nothing could be normal. He knew the motion that would be made, and he knew that he would grant it. To assemble the jurors for this seemed at first to be an unnecessary formality.

But he had decided that it was not a formality. He wasn't assembling the jurors again for the sake of this trial, or even for the sake of the system.

Yes, the Crown would offer counseling to them, and probably that would help; it was the least the Crown could do. But his sense of it was that this last meeting might do something immediately that would take counseling months or years to accomplish. It might offer closure.

But even if it didn't do that, it would at least give the court an opportunity to say what he wanted to say.

Ms. Sreenivasan—the same steward they'd had all along—opened the doors and called the jurors in. Nigel, Lucy, Mrs. Peabody, and Mr. Siger all filed in together, and took their seats in the primary jurors section, with the other surviving jurors. Eleven, in total.

The barristers for both sides were already present, and appeared to be as exhausted as Nigel felt. They were not squabbling, and they did not look as though they were about to.

McSweeney himself was present as well. Of all the people in the courtroom, he was the only one who seemed—well, happy.

A new bailiff called the court to order, and the judge entered. He sat down in a silent courtroom. He looked at the barristers. "Do you have a motion?" he said.

"We do, my lord," said Slattery. "The Crown moves for a mistrial."

"The defense concurs," said Langdon.

"It is so ordered," said the judge.

And then he turned to the jury. "Members of the jury," he began. "You may think the events that have transpired in this trial are extraordinary. And they are, of course. But many trials are extraordinary. I think it is fair to say that all trials are, if not extraordinary, at least profound, in the effects that they have on the parties involved. Nothing I have seen in the law is as extraordinary as the transformation that I see in jurors when they undertake their responsibilities. It happens every day. But I have never seen it happen to such an extent as I have seen in this jury. And so when I thank you now on behalf of the Crown, I want you to know that

I am thanking you for more than your service. I am thanking you for restoring my faith. Thank you."

And then he rapped his gavel. "Court is adjourned."

Ten minutes later, with the lawyers having already gone in their own directions, the jurors in the corridor began to slowly disperse. Four of them were dispersing more slowly than the others. There were two exits from the corridor, and they would be going in different directions, and they hesitated.

Mrs. Peabody spoke first, and she put her hands on theirs. "As I used to say to my late husband," she began, "if you'll indulge me this one last time—as I used to say to my late husband—I shall miss you very much."

She turned, her blue eyes shining, and went toward the stairs.

Siger stood with his pipe in his hand, unlit. He was staring at it. He was having trouble looking at Nigel and Lucy. Finally he did.

"I apologize if I caused either of you any concern by sneaking out that way in the middle of the night," he said. "I was reasonably certain there had to be a tunnel—there was really no other explanation for McSweeney being able to get back and forth to the mainland, unseen, to commit his murder. And I knew where the opening was, having actually tripped over it. It was arrogance on my part to go off exploring it secretly on my own while you all slept, I suppose, and for me to contact the authorities to set up the sting at the pub. I've been accused of that flaw before. In my youth, anyway. But also, I didn't want to put anyone else at risk. Ancient tunnels aren't the most predictable of places to

take a stroll, especially when you aren't equipped for spe-
lunking. With little light and no compass, it's easy to lose
your direction. Which, in fact I did. I was detoured in
off-branches of the main tunnel more than once, which
I regret—because otherwise I would have encountered the
bailiff on his way across."

"That's history," said Nigel. "What I want to know is,
will you go back to playing the violin?"

Siger smiled slightly and nodded. "My thanks to you
both," he said. "I will. But perhaps I'll do some other things
as well. It is, after all, every man's business to see justice
done." He turned and walked away down the corridor.

Now it was just Nigel and Lucy. She smiled—and then
spoke before he could, in a move that he knew was intended
to forestall any that he might make.

"You saw my tattoo, didn't you?"

"The England cricket team? Yes, I saw it."

"I was seventeen," she said, "and my first boyfriend was
a fan of the team, and I was a foolish fan of his. That's all
there was to that."

"I see."

"Do you want to see the other ones?"

"Other tattoos?"

"Yes."

"I most certainly do."

She pulled down the back edge of her halter top to ex-
pose an area just below the shoulder.

They were small, which was fine; it gave Nigel an excuse
to look closely.

A daisy. And a rose. Both the same size, next to each

other. Both appeared to be relatively recent, within the last few years.

Nigel thought about it. He thought about what Lois had said. The swimming lessons. The ballet lessons. And, what's more—the fact that even though Lucy clearly had the responsibility of taking someone to swimming lessons and ballet lessons, the court did not exempt her from jury duty.

"Daisy and Rose," said Nigel. "Your daughters."

"Twins," said Lucy with a laugh, and then she said, "And my husband and I are not divorced. Just disagreeing."

"So I gathered," said Nigel.

"Really? You did figure that out?"

Nigel nodded. "Of course," he said. "Elementary."

She kissed him on the cheek and then walked away down the hall.

## 27

At Bob's Newsstand on Baker Street, the headlines read, "McSweeney Will Play!"

"What do you think of that?" said Bob, as Nigel stopped for his morning coffee.

"Still can't say," said Nigel. "But at least I can listen to what you think of it now without concern."

"You want to know what I think of it?"

"If you want to say," said Nigel.

Bob shrugged. "Makes no difference to me. I'm not a betting man."

Nigel went on into the Dorset House lobby. He checked in with Mr. Hendricks, who was ecstatic. "Told you," said Hendricks.

"Yes, you did," said Nigel. "But they still might lose, you know."

Hendricks was immediately taken aback, and Nigel immediately wished he hadn't said it. It was cruel.

"But they won't," he added.

Nigel took the lift up to the chambers. Lois was at her desk. "So now you're back," she said.

"Yes. Any word from Reggie and Laura?"

"Reggie says they're taking another month."

"Ah."

"Which means the work is going to pile up around here. More court appearances than I can count. It seems to me we need another barrister in this chambers."

Nigel paused at her desk, and considered it. He nodded. "Yes," he said. "We'll see what can be done about that."

Epilogue

EIGHTEEN MONTHS LATER

At four in the morning at the McSweeney estate in Hampstead, the recently installed burglar alarm went off. Again.

In the master bedroom, Liam McSweeney woke, heard the ringing, and groaned. It was the fourth time this week. Every night, in fact, since the new system was installed. Always a false alarm.

He reached for the remote on the nightstand, found it, pressed it—but the little light didn't change color, and the ringing continued. The housekeeper had gone home. The butler had gone home. This was because McSweeney had made changes in the staffing; after the most recent mistrial—and the eventual dismissal of charges—he no longer felt comfortable having someone in the house who might snoop into god knows what. Things were going well, and he wanted to keep it that way.

So now he would have to go downstairs and shut the bloody thing off himself.

He was going to have some harsh words with the alarm company. They had come recommended by the local constabulary. He would let the local constabulary know, too, what he thought of their recommendation.

He walked down the wide circular staircase. He went to the kitchen and turned on the light. Everything was fine, everything was quiet—except for the ringing. He opened the cupboard where the control panel was installed, found the button, and pushed it.

The ringing stopped. The residual light from upstairs was glinting off something made of glass in the main hall. He paused.

The display cabinet was open. The display cabinet that held his cricket bat.

He'd had it cleaned, of course. And then he had put it back up. He'd told everyone that having it there did not remind him of his wife's unfortunate death at the hands of a burglar who was never caught; oh no. It reminded him of better times. And so he had put it back up. He had posed for a photo with it, his hand on the display case, looking back at the camera with an expression of both deep sorrow and a firm resolve to carry on.

And now the cabinet was open.

He took several steps toward it—and then he stopped, and stared, blinking, not quite comprehending, at the figure standing next to the case.

"You needn't have come," said McSweeney. "It's just

another false alarm, like all the others. I believe I made that clear when I called the station."

"Yes," said the police sergeant. "You did."

Now McSweeney saw that the sergeant had the cricket bat. He had taken it from the case. He was holding it almost as though he were about to step up and take his turn on a cricket pitch.

"It was my fault," said Sergeant Thackeray, very quietly. "I don't mean for the affair itself, although I take my share of that, too, of course. I mean the fact that you weren't convicted. If I had come forward when it counted—before it was too late—and acknowledged that she was indeed having an affair, and that it was with me—perhaps you would have been convicted. Although as the defense said, it still would have been a job to show that you actually knew about it."

McSweeney just stared, and the sergeant saw the surprise in his eyes.

"You didn't know it was me, did you? Clearly. But you did know about the affair. You found her letters. You read them. You burned them. And then you murdered her."

The sergeant paused on that for a moment. Then he continued. "You murdered her, and to protect my own career, I kept my mouth shut and let you get away with it."

The sergeant took a step closer to McSweeney, and said, "I've lived with that long enough. And so have you. I'll have to continue living with it. That will be my punishment."

The sergeant took one more step.

"This will be yours."

And then he swung the bat.